D1017306

The Lady Grace
Mysteries

From the Daybookes
of Lady Grace Cavendish

Book the Second

Betrayal

The Lady Grace Mysteries from Delacorte Press

ASSASSIN
BETRAYAL

THE
Lady
Grace
MYSTERIES

From the Daybookes
of Lady Grace Cavendish

BOOK THE SECOND

BETRAYAL

Patricia Finney is writing as Grace Cavendish

DELACORTE PRESS

Published by
Delacorte Press
an imprint of
Random House Children's Books
a division of Random House, Inc.
New York

Series created by Working Partners Ltd.
Text copyright © 2004 by Working Partners Ltd.

Visit us on the Web! www.randomhouse.com/kids
Educators and librarians, for a variety of teaching tools, visit us at
www.randomhouse.com/teachers

Library of Congress Cataloging-in-Publication Data
Cavendish, Grace.
Betrayal / Patricia Finney is writing as Grace Cavendish.
p. cm.—(The Lady Grace Mysteries, from the daybookes of Lady Grace Cavendish :
book the second)
Summary: Lady Grace Cavendish, Elizabeth I's youngest maid of honor, finds
herself in the midst of a battle at sea while posing as a boy aboard the ship of
Francis Drake, where she and Masou stowed away in hopes of finding
the kidnapped Lady Sarah.
ISBN 0-385-73152-3 (trade) — ISBN 0-385-90190-9 (GLB)
[1. Kings, queens, rulers, etc.—Fiction. 2. Great Britain—History—Elizabeth,
1558–1603—Fiction. 3. Kidnapping—Fiction. 4. Drake, Francis, Sir,
1540?–1596—Fiction. 5. Diaries—Fiction. 6. Mystery and detective stories.]
I. Title.
PZ7.F49825Be 2004
[Fic]—dc22
2003027053

The text of this book is set in 13-point Cloister.
Book design by Trish Parcell Watts
Printed in the United States of America
September 2004
10 9 8 7 6 5 4 3 2 1
BVG

To the real Jim Woolley—he knows who he is

MOST PRIVY AND SECRETE

DAYBOOKE THE SECOND

OF MY LADY GRACE CAVENDISH

AT THE MAIDS OF HONOUR, THEIR CHAMBER,

PALACE OF PLACENTIA

GREENWICH

ALL MISCREANTS AND ILL-THINKERS,

KEEP OUT1

Betrayal

Eventide

Now I am beginning my daybook the second—
the other is quite filled up. Today was very dull, sitting about winding wool for the Mistress of the
Maids, Mrs. Champernowne. At least there is something happening tomorrow—we accompany the
Queen to the docks at Tilbury. Very exciting! That
is why I am scribbling away and getting ink on my
smock, for I cannot sleep at all. Lady Sarah can't
sleep, either. She is writing a letter to her parents
bemoaning how poorly she is clad and how all her
raiment is utterly out of fashion.

At least the Queen sent me to walk the dogs this
afternoon. She has often given me that task since my
mother, the Queen's best friend, died a year ago,
God rest her soul, leaving me in Her Majesty's

care. I think she knows how much I enjoy playing with the dogs and spending time in the gardens, which I do, for that is where I find I am most reminded of my dear mother.

I changed into my horrible old hunting kirtle and then ran on tiptoes downstairs and along the painted passage to the door to the Privy Garden, where Mary Shelton was waiting with the dogs.

Now, I may like Mary Shelton better than I did— she has been very kind to me since my mother's passing. But I didn't want her getting nosy about what I do in the gardens—for I have a secret—so I invited her out with me. We raced up and down, with the dogs yapping away, and fairly soon she was red as an apple and puffing for breath.

"Oh Lord," she said, "I must go in and sit down."

"Are you sure?" I asked, putting my hand on her arm. "We could kick the ball for them again—"

"No, I need a rest," she insisted, fanning herself with her hand.

"Well, I'll run the dogs down to the Orchard," I told her. "I'll see you later."

Mary went inside, mopping her face. I can be quite cunning when necessary—not for nothing has the Queen appointed me her own Lady Pursuivant (for the pursuit and apprehension of all miscreants who trouble the Queen's peace at Court)!

I did run the dogs—throwing a stick for Henri, who is the chief of them despite being the smallest—and they all yelped madly. Then, when I was sure Mary couldn't see me, I slipped through the little gate into the Herb Garden. We have just moved to the Palace of Placentia at Greenwich, which is one of the Queen's most favourite residences. The palace gardens give right onto the river, and you can see the ducks and the swans and sometimes the pages and young henchmen fishing for salmon.

My friends Masou the tumbler and Ellie the laundrymaid have made a hidden place to sit inside the big yew hedge that surrounds the Herb Garden. And that's where I found Masou, who was sitting looking worried, but there was no sign of Ellie at all.

"She said she might be late," Masou explained. "The Deputy Laundress has her running about like a hunted rabbit."

Mrs. Twiste at the Whitehall laundry is a kind lady, but Mrs. Fadget, her deputy at Greenwich, is a nasty hag who loves to order poor Ellie about when we are at Placentia.

I settled down and watched Masou, who was idly

tossing red and green leather balls up and about his head. A bit of wood from the ground joined them, then a stone. It's amazing what Masou can do— turning somersaults in midair, juggling, and balancing. He's getting very big-headed because Mr. Somers—who's in charge of the tumblers—says he's so good. So I don't ever tell him, but I still like to watch.

We heard her cough first, then poor Ellie came dragging herself into the little hide and collapsed onto the ground next to me. She was coughing violently and her cheeks were flushed. I put my hand to her head as my mother used to do and it was all hot and dry.

"Ellie, you have a fever," I said.

"It's just that cold I had last week gone to my neck," she replied. Her throat sounded as if she had been eating sandpaper. "And that Mrs. Fadget"— she turned her head and spat—"I hate her. She had me up till past midnight wringing out sheets, and then up again at dawn to grate the soap. Then I was putting shirts on the hedge and I missed dinner. . . ."

I felt terrible. I usually bring Ellie something to eat and I'd forgotten. She saw me patting my pockets.

"It's all right," she said. "I ain't hungry a bit."

Masou and I looked at each other, feeling very worried now. Ellie! Not hungry? This was bad.

"You should be in bed, Ellie!" I told her. "You should be drinking horrible willow-bark tinctures and sniffing the smoke of henbane of Peru."

Ellie laughed. "Tell Mrs. Fadget," she said. "What's 'appening tomorrow? The Queen's watermen were moaning down at the buttery about how early they've got to get up."

"The Queen's going to Tilbury," I explained. "And we're going with her to see the Royal Dockyards."

"Oh. And will you put it in your daybooke?" Ellie asked curiously.

"Of course," I replied.

"Wish I could do that. Write, I mean," Ellie went on wistfully.

"Well, you can read," I pointed out.

"Only my name. But all the things I see—and the stories I hear in the laundry," she croaked. "I wish I could write them down."

"You could tell me and I could write them in my tongue," suggested Masou helpfully.

"No good to me, I can't read that, neither," Ellie

said, and sighed. "I wish I could read them ballad sheets. Or I could save up all my pennies and maybe, one day, even buy a book and read it!"

My chest felt all tight and heavy. Ellie's voice sounded so sad, as if actually *buying* a book was a mountain she could never hope to climb—and the Queen *gives* them to me! I put my arm round Ellie. "I wish I could have you as my tiring woman instead of sharing Olwen or Fran with the other girls, but the Queen keeps forgetting."

"What I really want is a good sleep," muttered Ellie, and coughed and wrapped her thin arms around herself. Masou took his jerkin off and bundled it up for a pillow to her head. She lay down with a sigh and Masou very softly sang her one of his funny wailing little songs.

Poor Ellie, it is so unfair—she has to keep working even when she's ill, while I have the Queen's own physician to tend me if I so much as sniffle! And I hardly ever get ill anyway. Mind, I don't have to forage around for food, or work till midnight on cold, wet sheets—I'm sure that has something to do with it.

I left them there and came back to the Privy Garden, where I found Mary Shelton wandering about looking all upset.

"Where did you go?" she demanded. "I was looking for you in the Orchard but you weren't there."

"Yes I was," I said quickly. "I was up a tree."

"Oh," she replied, and stopped looking so nosy—Mary doesn't like climbing trees. "Well, the Queen wants you."

When I reached the Queen, I found that she wanted me to help brush her hair this evening—which I like doing despite having to be so careful of the tangles in her curls. She snaps and swears if you pull even slightly and her hair is naturally quite frizzy, so it knots. She is talking about having the whole lot cut off and wearing a wig instead!

I'd better get to bed now. Writing this has made me sleepy—and we've got an early start tomorrow.

Dark before dawn . . .

Now I have but a few moments to write a little—
there! A first blot, too. I can't help it, the sun is not
yet up and my candle is small.

We have all arisen early to accompany Her
Majesty on her visit to Tilbury—where King
Henry's old naval yards are. Her Majesty has been
entreated to visit the yards by Mr. John Hawkins, a
most notable seafarer and merchant to the New
World, whose passion for all things naval seems to
know no bounds! He is making suit for the office of
Secretary to the Admiralty as he has great plans for
the Navy. The Queen finds him charming and has
agreed to hear him. And he has assured her that we
shall have no need to be afeared of bawdy sailors
during our visit. Fie!

I am not sure where Tilbury is, but we are travelling there by boat, which is exciting, except I will be wearing my third-best gown—the russet woollen one with the velvet trimmings—and pray it is not splashed too much.

Lady Sarah's tiring woman, Olwen, has almost finished squeezing Lady Sarah into her white Court damask. We have been told to wear our third-best clothes, but Lady Sarah is insisting on her best kirtle.

Mary Shelton has just whispered to me, "Somebody hopes for a handsome sailor."

Lady Sarah heard us giggling and has just told us to shut up. She is still moaning about having to rise so early. Hell's teeth! She is applying more of that foul-smelling ointment to the spot on her chin—Clown's All-Heal and woodlice mashed together, I think. I wish I had a stopper for my nose.

Time to end—Olwen is coming over to help me with my stays.

Later this Day—eventide

What a day this has been! *So* exciting and unusual. I shall carry on where I left off:

9

Once Olwen had laced me into my stays, I pulled on my outdoor boots and struggled to get my kirtle straight over my bumroll—I didn't bother with a farthingale because I thought I might have a chance to explore a ship or something, and anyway, the kirtle's a bit short for me and it shows less if I don't wear a farthingale. Olwen then tackled my hair, which, as she is first to say, is hardly my best feature, being rather fine and mousy. She decided to hide as much of it as she could under a sweet green velvet hat with a feather.

I then rushed into the passageway, where Mrs. Champernowne was standing tapping her foot and sighing, as we were all late.

Lady Sarah emerged resplendent in her gown, and Mrs. Champernowne tutted.

"Did you not hear my message, Lady Sarah?" she asked. "We will be taking the Queen's galley down to Tilbury and the damask is sure to be splashed by the water, look you, and be all spoiled and spotted and spattered."

Lady Sarah only tossed her head and said, "I am in need of new apparel. This English-cut bodice is last year's fashion, so of no great moment."

It's all French cut and doublet-style this year—but

I don't call a year particularly old for a whole kirtle and bodice. And I know for a fact that Lady Sarah has five kirtles and any number of stomachers and sleeves and false fronts and petticoats. In fact, most of the mess in our bedchamber consists of Lady Sarah's clothes. Who needs five kirtles? I know the Queen has hundreds but she's the Queen. The Wardrobe is a Department of State, after all!

We'd already eaten breakfast in our chambers, so Mrs. Champernowne led us down the stairs and along the Painted Passage, all holding candles and yawning fit to burst.

The Queen was just leaving her Withdrawing Chamber, with the Chamberers still pinning her bodice. She had chosen brocade-trimmed black wool, so everyone who was wearing silk or velvet looked worried, and serve them right: silk or velvet shows water splashes even more than good wool, and any fool should know better than to out-dress the Queen.

We passed through the palace and into the garden. Torches were burning all the way down the watersteps to where the Queen's galley was waiting. The harbingers and trumpeters were already in rowing boats and wherries, while the Gentlemen of the

Guard, in their red velvet, were climbing into gigs. It was funny to watch them cursing each other: they were having trouble fitting their long halberds into the narrow boats that were to carry them.

The Queen's galley is very handsome—all silver-gilt and red paint—and rowed by the Queen's Boatmen, ten of them, who wear red and black livery and a badge. Some of the other Maids of Honour were nudging each other and pointing out the good-looking ones.

We all had to climb in before the Queen. It wasn't easy getting into a boat that wobbled underneath me, especially when I couldn't see my feet for my petticoats and I couldn't really bend in the middle because of my stays. The Chief Boatman steadied each of us with his arm, and at last we were all sitting down, two by two, along the middle of the boat.

As usual, the Queen had asked one of her favourite gentlemen, Mr. Christopher Hatton, to accompany her. He helped Her Majesty to board, and once the Queen was settled on the cushions under her canopy, the oarsmen pushed off and started to row.

The sun was just coming up and turning the river silver-grey and gold. Every bit of the Thames was full of boats, and wherries with red lateen sails, and gigs, and Thames ferryboats—and little private craft, all overloaded with people. The courtiers still on the watersteps were politely fighting over the few remaining craft, and the boatmen were asking shocking amounts to take them.

I loved it. There was quite a strong wind so I had to hold onto my hat, but it was so exciting to be skimming the water and rocking a bit as the oarsmen bent to the stroke. I always love going by boat. I wanted to trail my fingers in the water, feel how cold it was, but I couldn't reach past the gilded carving on the side, and Mrs. Champernowne was glaring at me something horrid. A swan flapped its wings and honked at her, probably because it didn't like the look on her face, either.

Lady Jane Coningsby and Lady Sarah ignored each other pointedly for the whole journey. Lady Jane has only lately come to Court. Another Maid of Honour, Katharine Broke, went home in disgrace after a scandal with the Duke of Norfolk's nephew, and so Lady Jane arrived to make the number of Maids of Honour up to six again. It's as good as a play to watch her with Lady Sarah because the two of them hate each other so. Lady Sarah has beautiful red hair—like the Queen's, but less inclined to frizz—whereas Lady Jane has wonderful blond curls "foaming down her back," as one of the dafter Court gentlemen wrote in a poem. Lady Sarah has more womanly curves than Lady Jane, but Lady Jane is taller and more elegant. The worst of it is that they always like exactly the same gentlemen!

When we reached Tilbury there was a strong smell of paint. Most of the houses had been newly whitewashed in honour of the Queen's visit—rather badly, as they all had splatters on their shutters. A crowd had gathered at the side of the muddy road, and litters were ready and waiting next to the Gentlemen of the Guard, who were all lined up.

As we climbed laboriously out of the galley and up the steps, Lady Sarah nearly tripped on a bit of rope.

"Do try and watch where you're going, Lady Sarah," sniffed Lady Jane.

Oh, how pink Lady Sarah's cheeks went! And her "rosebud lips" tightened into a thin line.

Then, as Lady Jane was herself being helped ashore, a wave from a nearby boat, overloaded with courtiers, made the galley dip suddenly. She would have fallen in the water if the Queen's Oarsman had not caught her!

"Dear, dear," said Lady Sarah loudly from the

quay. "*Somebody* had a bit too much beer at break-fast."

"I bet you sixpence that Jane slaps Sarah first," whispered Mary Shelton at my elbow, her eyes shining.

I thought about this. Lady Sarah has fiery red hair and a temper to match. "Done!" I declared. "Sixpence on it." We shook hands.

The Queen often rides side-saddle in processions, but today she had ordered a litter with a canopy over it to shade her from the sun or keep the rain off her (far more likely!). I was praying we wouldn't have to ride and, thank goodness, there were litters for us as well. We climbed in, arguing over who should sit in front. But while the rest of us were quarrelling, Lady Sarah had pushed her way to the front of one litter, and Lady Jane established herself at the front of the other, looking very elegant and aloof. Grumbling, the rest of us crammed in behind, then the littermen hoisted us up, and off we went.

As is usual when the Queen goes anywhere, it was quite a procession. The harbingers and trumpeters led the way with the Royal Standard, blasting away on their trumpets, banging drums and shouting, "The Queen! The Queen! Make way for the

Queen's Majesty!" It wasn't really necessary, because the people looked as if they had been camping out all night to see the Queen, but it did serve to wake a couple who were still asleep, wrapped in blankets, as we went past.

After the trumpeters marched half the Gentlemen of the Guard in their red velvet, carrying their halberds and looking miserable because their smart red hose was getting badly splashed with mud. Then came the Queen in her litter, then more Gentlemen of the Guard, then us, then the courtiers, and, at the very back, boys and dogs running along, shouting and barking.

Everybody was waving and cheering, and the Queen was smiling and waving back and blowing kisses. It's wonderful to watch her whenever she processes anywhere. She lights up and seems somehow bigger and more Queenly—and she never minds how muddy the road is or how smelly the people might be (though she might complain about it afterwards).

A little girl ran out with a posy of flowers for her. But as Mr. Hatton reached out to take it from her, the Queen stopped him and gave an order for the procession to stop. Mr. Hatton then dismounted and lifted the little girl up for the Queen herself to take flowers from her sticky, outstretched paw. The Queen then gave the little girl a kiss. All the people roared at that. The Queen pinned the posy to her bodice with a flourish.

I watched Mr. Hatton put the little girl back down on the ground. She curtsied and then, with a shining face, rushed back to tell her mamma and grandmamma all about it.

Her Majesty then smiled and waved and bowed as the procession moved on.

Mrs. Champernowne sighed. She was uncomfortably squashed in next to me at the back of the litter. "Tut. We'll be needing to burn a stick of incense inside that bodice to have all the fleas and lice and nits out of it now," she moaned.

We eventually arrived at the dockyards, where they build merchantmen to sail to Spain and New Spain and the Netherlands, and France and Muscovy. All the workmen were lined up in front of the ships, wearing their Sunday best to meet the Queen.

Mr. Hatton helped the Queen down from her litter. Mr. John Hawkins was there to greet her. I recognized him from the time he had come to Court to ask the Queen, personally, to visit her Royal Dockyards.

"Oh!" Lady Sarah gasped in front.

Mary Shelton and I craned our necks to see if anybody was slapping anybody.

Typical Lady Sarah: she was simpering and batting her eyelashes because there were two handsome young men standing behind Mr. Hawkins. One was tall with fair hair and a slightly receding chin. The other was shorter and broader, with a cheerful round face and disarmingly bright blue eyes. They looked to be good friends for I caught the shorter one exchanging appreciative looks with the taller one, who winked back.

"Your Majesty," said Mr. Hawkins, "may I present Captain Hugh Derby?" The tall man bowed low. "And Captain Francis Drake." It was the stockier one's turn.

The Queen let them kiss her hand and then stepped onto the planks they had put down to preserve her from the mud. She walked along the line of workmen as they all doffed their blue statute caps and bowed. Mr. Hawkins moved along beside the Queen, introducing and explaining.

Mrs. Champernowne beckoned Mary and me forward to help with the Queen's train, which was wider than the walkway she was standing on.

"Hold it high, the mud is terrible!" growled the Queen. Then she glanced at Lady Sarah and Lady Jane. "Whatever are those two ninnies at now?" she snapped, frowning at them.

I looked at the two ninnies. Lady Jane had a very haughty expression on her face, in spite of the fact that she had her foot in a muddy puddle. It was a pity she was wearing such a pretty pair of high-heeled shoes with pompoms on the front, because one heel now appeared to be stuck. And Lady Sarah had somehow caught her petticoat on a bit of wood. Captain Drake and Captain Derby were practically bumping heads as they tried to unsnag it, both of them quite ignoring Lady Jane.

We walked on through a very battered and splintered gate. It had the Royal Coat of Arms carved above it, but the paint and gilt was all cracked and peeling. We were entering a dockyard. There were no ships, just empty pits where they would have been built and which would then have been filled with Thames water to launch them. Some old bits of wood lay scattered about, and a coil of rope was being used as a nest by seagulls.

The Queen stopped dead and looked around, her hands on her hips. "Good God! What a desolation. Why has this happened?"

"No money, Your Majesty," burred Mr. Hawkins. "No money and no interest. And what's more, all the ships your Royal Father built are near ready to sink from shipworm."

The Queen was frowning. "I had no idea. And I pay thousands of pounds every year to the Royal Dockyards for the fitting out of my warships."

Mr. Hawkins didn't say anything to this, only stared into space.

The Queen's frown became positively menacing. I would hate to be whoever is Secretary of the Navy at the moment.

Mary Shelton nudged me. I looked to where she was pointing and saw that Lady Jane now had her muddy foot firmly on the back of Lady Sarah's damask kirtle, where it would leave a nice clear imprint. Her face was pure innocence, of course.

"I'm going to win when Sarah sees that," I whispered to Mary. "Hope you've got sixpence to pay me."

"Lady Jane will snap first," Mary insisted. "Look at her face."

It was true that Lady Jane was looking very sour,

but I know how fussy Sarah is over her gowns. "We shall see," I replied.

We moved on, with Mr. Hawkins still talking and talking. Mary and I had to hurry forward because the Queen was walking briskly and we had to make sure her train didn't fall in the mud. As we passed Lady Sarah I saw her staring at the muddy footprint on her white damask.

Next thing, Lady Sarah "accidentally" gave Lady Jane a shove with her bumroll, and Lady Jane stepped off the walkway, getting her other pretty high-heeled shoe stuck in the mud.

By now Mr. Hawkins had the crook of his arm held out for Her Majesty to lean on. Mr. Hatton followed behind, looking as if his nose was thoroughly put out of joint.

"Well, you see, Your Majesty," Hawkins was saying enthusiastically, "what we need is a new kind of ship altogether—a lower ship, with no castles and smooth hulls, built for speed—"

"Mr. Hawkins," the Queen interrupted, putting out her white kid-gloved hand to stop him.

Hawkins, Drake, and Derby blinked at her.

She smiled. "Gentlemen, I speak excellent French, Italian, and Latin, not to mention English, but alas, I have absolutely no Sailorish." Then she pointed at a docked galleon. "Those are the castles?" she asked, pointing at the raised ends of the ship.

"Aye," Mr. Hawkins confirmed. "They're used for boarding, Ma'am," he explained. "Being higher than an enemy ship makes it easier to board from them. One can just drop down onto the deck of another ship."

"Ah. I see," the Queen acknowledged. "Then should not our ships have higher castles than the enemy's—else what happens if the enemy boards from his high castles?"

Hawkins grinned and winked down at her. "He'm got to catch us first, Ma'am, which he won't if we have the fastest ships."

"But how do you know your new lower ships will be faster?" the Queen inquired.

"I know it because God made fish for to swim fast and I learned the shape from Him," declared Mr. Hawkins simply.

"The argument is sound," agreed the Queen, nodding. "But can you prove it?"

"Aye, Your Majesty," Hawkins said. "Captain Drake has an amusement for you and your Court if you'll come this way." His expression reminded me of my friend Masou when he is about to pull off a spectacular trick.

We all processed along a walkway covered with canvas to a pool like a big rectangular fishpond. There were two winches with handles at one end and two rollers at the other. Floating on the water, held by ropes that went round the rollers and back to the winches, were two beautifully made model ships.

A chair stood on a dais under an awning for the Queen to take her ease upon, which she did, while Mary and I arranged her train.

Captain Drake stepped forward and his sharp blue eyes sparkled as he talked about the models. "This one here is the exact shape of a Spanish galleon, Your Majesty. Do you see how high her castles are and how round her hull? We based her on a ship I took two summers ago." He moved to the other model ship, which looked much less magnificent. "Now, this one here is a kind of ship that does not even exist yet, although my own ship, the *Judith,* has a hull not so very unlike it. This is what you might call a race-built galleon and the trick's in her hull, which is long and narrow and smooth like a dolphin."

The Queen nodded. "And the winches?" she asked.

"Ah, that's for the wager." He waved forward two sturdy young men. "Now, here are Jem and Michael that are 'prenticed shipwrights and built strong, as you can see. Do you think they could turn the winch quickly?"

Everybody nodded, fascinated to know what he would say next. "Well, I say that the English race-built galleon can beat the Spanish galleon, even if two of the Queen's own gentlewomen are turning the winch for it! In fact I'll wager ten shillings on it. Who'll take my bet?"

Well, the Court gentlemen thought this hysterically funny and, to be truthful, so did we, because the two young shipwrights looked as if they knew a thing or two about turning a winch. Mr. Hatton stepped forward at once to take Captain Drake's bet and so did some of the other gentlemen. But I noticed that Captain Derby simply grinned at his friend and made no move to gamble. The Queen watched and smiled.

"Now, ladies, who shall turn the English galleon's winch?" asked Captain Drake of all of us.

Nobody said anything at first because we were all still giggling and murmuring amongst ourselves. But then I decided to step forward, because it certainly looked an interesting activity. To my astonishment, Lady Sarah stepped forward, too, dropped a curtsy, and said, "I'll do it, too."

The Queen blinked in surprise and then gestured us over. Lady Jane smirked at the girl next to her—and then looked sour when she saw the rapt expression on Drake's face, as he stared at Lady Sarah. I thought Captain Derby looked fairly stupid as well. And the two shipwrights seemed as stunned as rabbits facing a fox at the sight of a damask-clad, red-curled lady of the Court advancing on them, pulling on her gloves.

I hurried after her, only I'd forgotten my gloves so I had to manage without.

"Ready, steady, go!" cried Captain Derby.

The shipwrights started turning their winch, which gradually wound in the rope attached to the Spanish galleon model and pulled their ship through the water.

Sarah and I had a bit of trouble because Sarah was trying to turn the winch one way and I was turning the other, but once we sorted that out, and the English race-built galleon started being pulled through the water, too, it was easy. We even caught up with the Spanish galleon because our ship moved more easily through the water—then fell back a bit because we were still arguing. But then, with everyone spurring us on, we stopped talking, turned the winch together, and our ship got to the other side of the pond first!

Everyone cheered and clapped, and Lady Sarah curtsied prettily, standing in front of me so that Captain Drake would get the full benefit of her breathlessness as he settled up with Mr. Hatton.

"Very impressive indeed, Captain Drake," said the Queen, still laughing and dabbing her eyes with a handkerchief. "And I lost a shilling to Mr. Hawkins, backing your strong young shipwrights—I should have had more faith."

We then continued to another quay, where a very narrow two-masted ship was moored. We went up the gangplank, handed along by pigtailed sailors, and there on the deck was a table laid with a magnificent feast! A big, sullen-looking boy was sitting in the ropes above, waving a rattle to keep the seagulls away.

I could feel the ship rocking gently on the water. I thought it was quite a pleasant, soothing motion but some of the other girls looked a little queasy. The Queen didn't mind, though. She sat in a chair with the Cloth of Estate over it and the rest of us sat wherever we liked. Lady Sarah laughed as prettily as a silver bell when Captain Drake brought her a plate of little pies and carven potherbs. I looked away—it was quite sick-making.

That was when I noticed a mouse pottering gently along the deck beside the rail, its little nose quivering at the smell of all the food laid on the table. Nobody likes rats, but I don't mind mice—although I'm probably the only Maid of Honour *ever* who isn't terrified of them. I elbowed Mary to look because I didn't want her to miss the fun.

Sure enough, as Lady Sarah caught sight of the mouse she let out a terrible shriek, jumped up, and stood teetering on her bench, squealing like a stuck pig.

Lady Jane sneered; then, when she saw what Sarah was staring at, she screamed as well. Everybody else shrieked for all they were worth, except me and Mary—who doesn't like mice but has some sense. And the Queen and the men, of course.

Captain Drake spun on his heel, his hand flying to his sword. Then he took in Lady Sarah perched on the bench, pulling her skirts around her, and the mouse looking curiously up at her, whiskers twitching. In one movement he swept off his velvet cap and threw it over the mouse.

"What in God's name . . . !" bellowed the Queen.

"Only a little waif, Your Majesty," said Drake. He went over and picked up his hat with its little captive and showed the mouse to the Queen. Then he turned to Lady Sarah and said in his soft Devon burr, "Will I kill it for you, my lady, or let it go?"

Lady Sarah's cheeks were very pink. "Thank you for rescuing me, Captain," she gasped. "But please don't kill it."

Drake bowed, went to the side of the ship nearest the dock, and emptied out the mouse and its droppings onto dry land.

The Queen smiled and clapped, so we all did, too. "Well thrown, Captain!" she declared. "What excellent aim. Do you play at bowls?"

"I like a game now and then, Your Majesty," Drake replied, smiling.

"Then you must teach *me* to throw straight," said the Queen. "Alas, it is an art I have never yet mastered."

"Which is just as well when she's throwing a slipper at us!" I muttered to Mary, who snickered.

"If it can be done, Your Majesty, I will do it," said Drake tactfully, and he bowed to the Queen and again to Lady Sarah, who had sat down gracefully on her bench once more.

Neither Captain Drake nor Captain Derby seemed to mind Sarah's being such a ninny. Drake fetched her more food while Derby fetched her more wine. Drake called on the minstrels at the back of the ship to play a tune she liked, while Derby showed her a brilliantly coloured bird with a big beak that came from New Spain, and liked to sit on his shoulder and eat nuts. He called it a popinjay. Then Drake started pointing to bits of the ship, like the ropes and the mast, telling her the proper names.

Lady Jane was watching all this and scowling. Suddenly she gulped and ran to the side of the ship, looking quite green. Then she leaned over and was sick.

"Oh dear," moaned Mary, stumbling to the side herself and doing the same.

"They say an eel's tail eaten raw and no beer for a week will settle an ailing stomach, dear Lady Jane," Sarah said happily. Then she turned to Captain Drake. "I love ships," she said, simpering. "My uncle took me on one of his merchant venturers when I was small and I even climbed up those rope ladders there to the little platform thing. My father was quite shocked when he found out."

"Ah, you climbed the ratlines to the fighting top," murmured Drake, seeming fascinated by Sarah's revelation. "How clever of you!"

Sarah looked delighted. "The Ship's Master

offered to take me as a cabin boy, when I was older—until my uncle explained who I was," she confided. "I was quite a tomboy back then."

I nudged Mary at this because I couldn't imagine it at all. And seeing Captain Drake's eyes stray back down to Sarah's chest, I could see he was having trouble imagining it, too. But poor Mary didn't smile. She was holding her stomach and looking unhappy. In fact, I think me and Lady Sarah and the sailors were the only ones who really enjoyed that meal.

Afterwards, it was time for us to go back ashore, which felt very strange for a minute. Now that the tide was high enough, they had brought the galley round to collect the Queen from the dockside, so we went straight over from the quay to the main water-steps.

The crowd was waiting to wave us goodbye as we climbed into the galley. Her Majesty was already under her awning, waving and smiling again when it happened: as Lady Sarah picked up her skirts, ready to climb aboard, a rope that had been lying on the ground suddenly tightened against her leg. She swayed, wobbled, waved her arms like a Dutch windmill—and fell over the side of the watersteps, right into the Thames!

There was pandemonium. Everyone ran about. Sarah threshed her arms in the water and screamed like a banshee. I observed that Lady Jane was staring innocently into space—right next to the other end of the rope. But nobody else had noticed because they were all either squalling or shouting advice.

Next moment, there was the sound of running feet. Captain Drake pounded by, stripping off his doublet and sword belt as he went, then he jumped into the muddy water in his shirt and hose.

Sarah's skirts were dragging her down and she was screaming and spluttering dreadfully. She grabbed Captain Drake when he reached her and they both went under. When they surfaced, Sarah seemed a bit dazed. Drake had her caught from behind, with his arm around her neck. He pulled her steadily over to the dock wall. Hawkins was there, passing down a rope on a pulley. Drake quickly tied it in a complicated way around Lady Sarah's waist and shoulders and then shouted to the shipwrights on the quay to haul on the rope. Up came Sarah out of the water, covered in weed and looking like a drowned rat. Captain Drake shouted something else, caught another rope, and used it to walk up the wall in a rather dashing way, so that he was on shore, ready to catch the half-fainting Lady Sarah in his arms, as the men winched her down again.

Mrs. Champernowne was there, too, with a shawl and a pair of snips to cut Lady Sarah's stay laces so she could breathe properly.

I gave Lady Jane another hard stare, but by then she was nowhere near the rope that had tripped Sarah, so I couldn't say anything. Lady Sarah was in a terrible state, and though she does exaggerate, I think being half-drowned is enough to upset anyone! Her damask gown and her stays were ruined of course, and, while she had taken no real hurt from the muddy water, she was very cold and wet.

Captain Drake carried Sarah aboard the Queen's galley, where he laid her on some cushions. Mrs. Champernowne chafed Sarah's hands and thanked him very graciously. The Queen, who had witnessed the drama, summoned the Captain. As he kneeled before her, she said, "Thank you for saving the life of our Maid of Honour, Captain Drake. Devon must breed very quick-thinking men."

"Aye, Your Majesty," Captain Drake responded. "If we are not quick of thought, the sea takes us. And it was an honour to assist one of your ladies."

The Queen smiled, pleased with the answer, and held out her hand so he could kiss it.

"Please, Ma'am," ventured Drake, "may I have the greater honour of attending Your Majesty even unto Greenwich?"

The Queen nodded her assent. "To be sure, Captain, you are all most welcome to return to Court with us," she said, "for I have more to discuss with Mr. Hawkins."

We could not leave at once because there was still more fuss to be made over Lady Sarah. A boy from the ship was called and sent running to fetch aqua vitae and a blanket from the Captain's own bed. By the time Sarah was settled, Captain Drake had returned in dry clothes, with only his hair still wet. He looked very dashing, and after his impressive rescue of Lady Sarah, several of the other girls were looking at her quite enviously.

We finally set off. As the oarsmen rowed upstream, Hawkins carried on telling the Queen his plans for the Navy. Captain Derby sat astern, staring thoughtfully at his friend, while Captain Drake sat next to Lady Sarah, agreeing with Mrs. Champernowne that a hot toddy of aqua vitae, honey, citron, and water—with a good sprinkling of nutmeg and cinnamon—would be the best medicine for her.

Mary and I had a bit of an argument about our

bet, but as Lady Jane hadn't actually *slapped* Sarah, nobody had won.

When we arrived at the Greenwich Palace water-steps, Captain Drake swept Sarah up in his arms and carried her all the way to the Queen's own bathroom, where she could have a hot bath. My uncle, Dr. Cavendish, was also called to open the vein in Sarah's left arm in order to guard against infection.

She seems much happier now, and Captain Drake will be staying at Court tonight to see how she is in the morning.

What an exciting day! Everybody is gossiping about Captain Drake and Lady Sarah. I can't wait to see what happens tomorrow.

Morning, at Greenwich

I truly think Captain Drake is in love with Lady Sarah! He is certainly paying court to her. This very morning he sent her a posy of flowers tied up by a pearl bracelet—and a note with it that made her pink. As I write, Sarah is holding up her hand to admire the jewel and singing the praises of the Captain. She really seems quite smitten!

But Hell's teeth! I can scarcely think of a worse match for her. Everyone knows he is no rich lord, but a Devon pirate who has made some money on a voyage lately, and is spending it on his ship faster than a Spaniard home from the New World. Her parents will surely beat her if they find out she is dallying with anyone but a rich courtier. Lady Sarah may think she is safe enough with them a hundred miles away in the north at Bartelmy Hall, but someone will surely be nosy enough to write and tell them. And no parents in the world would countenance a fifteen-year-old heiress's flirting with a sea captain! They are seeking a good match for her now.

Mrs. Champernowne has just come in and, seeing Lady Sarah so lively, she said, "Well now, I think you are as fit as a fiddle, so out of bed with you, and back to your duties." And for a wonder, Sarah has not moaned at how hard-hearted she is.

Fie! Mrs. Champernowne has just told me to stop my scribbling as well. I am to change into my second-best kirtle—the white damask. I expect we are wanted to sit in the Presence Chamber and wind wool for Mrs. Champernowne while Her Majesty talks to tedious Scottish ambassadors and the like.

Later this Day

Well, this morning has been far more interesting than I thought it would be. (It's a good thing I carry my daybooke in my embroidery workbag, along with a penner full of pens and ink. Mrs. Champernowne thinks it would be more improving for me to sew in odd moments than scribble, but the Queen allows it.)

It took an age to ready myself for the Queen's Presence Chamber, as my hair simply refused to cooperate. No sooner had one lock been pinned up than another fell down. Why does hair do that some days? For once, even Lady Sarah was ready before me. Finally, I had my damask on and my hair dressed with my rope of pearls through it, and I rushed to the Presence Chamber.

Thank the Lord, the Queen was not there when I puffed in and sat down. Lady Sarah had already arrived and taken my favourite cushion, so I had to have the small hard one. She is clearly quite recovered! I noticed that she had Captain Drake's posy pinned to her bodice and the pearl bracelet on her right wrist. She and Lady Jane were sitting with their backs to each other like sulking cats, as usual.

"Where is the Queen?" I asked, squeezing in next to plump Mary Shelton. "What did I miss?" I could see her face was pink with the effort of not laughing.

"Her Majesty has withdrawn before she gives audience to Mr. Hawkins. She is very annoyed with Lady Sarah and Lady Jane," Mary whispered. "Lady Sarah came in and accidentally on purpose trod on the edge of Lady Jane's kirtle and it ripped a bit. . . . And Sarah said, 'Oh dear, not very well-made, is it? Perhaps I could recommend you a good tailor?' And then Lady Jane said, 'I know you can't help your clumsiness, dear Lady Sarah, because you can't see where your feet are going . . .' And then the Queen threw one shoe at Lady Jane and one at Lady Sarah and told them to stop squabbling like a pair of geese!"

Just then, there was a flourish of trumpets and four of the Gentlemen of the Queen's Guard came in and stood there looking handsome with their halberds, which is their job. The Queen swept in, wearing black velvet and white samite, and we saw that Mr. Hawkins was with her, attended by the two Captains.

As he passed, Captain Drake nodded and smiled at Lady Sarah, and she looked very pleased with herself. Unlike Lady Jane, who looked like she had sucked a lemon.

"My dear Mr. Hawkins," said the Queen in the sort of ringing voice she uses for public announcements that are pretending to be private, "we are so grateful to you for showing us the state of our Royal Father's naval yards and docks. For otherwise we might have gone on for years being cozened out of our Navy, whereas now we most truly intend to make repair and rebuild all that has gone to rack and ruin."

Right on cue, Hawkins, Drake, and Derby kneeled.

"Now, it would be against all right dealing, and clean contrary to precedent, for us to make the sweeping changes that you have been urging, but we can at least make a start. We shall cause to have painted a portrait of our Royal Self, with ships and docks in the background, as it were in signal of our loving watchfulness for the Navy."

I caught Drake and Derby exchanging glances, looking very disappointed. In fact, Drake rolled his eyes. Luckily the Queen didn't see.

"We shall also begin to reform the docks themselves. Or rather, you shall, Mr. Hawkins. For by this patent I hereby make you Counsel Extraordinary to the Navy until the post of Secretary becomes vacant."

Mr. Hawkins bowed low. "Your Majesty shall find me the best adviser—"

"All in good time, Mr. Hawkins," the Queen interrupted impatiently. "For the moment, please continue as you have done, and by all means make friends among the shipwrights. But wait until you have the Secretaryship before you make changes, do you understand?"

"I am certain to have the Secretaryship?" Mr. Hawkins asked, sounding delighted.

"As soon as the greedy idle fat pudding of a man

who has it now consents to die or step down," said the Queen with a ferocious smile. "But all must be done smoothly and politically or the Royal Docks will end up the worse for it."

Hawkins smiled back and nodded. "Aye, Your Majesty, it shall be as you say."

"Excellent. That is all for now." And Her Majesty dismissed Mr. Hawkins and the two Captains.

I have finished my recording just in time—it is midday, and the Maids of Honour are to eat dinner with the Queen in the Parlour.

Later this Day

Hell's teeth! Lady Sarah too is surely in love! There she was at dinner time, sighing and picking at her food because *Somebody* was having to eat in the Great Hall and wasn't there! But she soon perked up when Her Majesty decided to invite Mr. Hawkins and the two Captains to partake of some afternoon air with us in the Privy Garden.

As we walked, Mr. Hawkins continued to expound on ships to Her Majesty. I could see she was listening with interest, but I'm not sure she understood all he was saying because there were so many Sailorish words mixed up in it. I certainly didn't! So I decided to listen in on some easier conversation.

Lady Sarah had, rather rudely, drawn Mary Shelton's attention from Lady Jane to moan to her about the disaster that had happened to her gown the day before. "What I need is a sixteen-yard dress-length of that lovely white samite and some pearls to put with it," she said. Mary nodded politely. "The damask is utterly ruined—it's too bad even to give to Olwen," Sarah went on. "And I *desperately* need a French-cut bodice and a new ruff and some black-worked sleeves and a new petticoat, and even my bumroll smells of river water now so I must throw it away. . ."

"If I can take a fat Flemish merchanter, shall I bring you the booty to make you a new gown?" asked Captain Drake, who had overheard this, as he was supposed to.

Sarah blushed—and I knew why: it would have been more seemly for him to beg the Queen to give Lady Sarah the samite, like a proper courtier, than to go round capturing ships for it! But he didn't seem to know that—and his offer was very romantic. Lady Sarah looked quite charmed by this blatant display of his regard.

"I could do that, too," put in Captain Derby hopefully.

Sarah ignored him. "But I thought only the Spaniards had treasure," she said, simpering up at Drake and fluttering her eyelashes.

"The Flemish are Spanish Netherlanders," Drake explained, "and worth the spoiling, for they carry bolts and bolts of silk and velvet."

"Oh, Captain Drake, then could you capture me a Flemish merchanter with plenty of samite and velvet? And then could you capture me a big Spanish galleon loaded with pearls—like the ones in my lovely bracelet?" Sarah wheedled, with her head on one side and her jewelled wrist held up prettily—quite disgusting to see, really.

"Aye, with a glad heart." Drake laughed and bowed. "Anything my lady desires."

Mary Shelton, who had of course overheard this exchange, elbowed me and made a sick face at all this romantic talk.

The Queen called Sarah over to her then, and the Captains walked off, oh so casually, in the same direction.

I am almost beginning to feel sorry for Captain Derby: he will persist—but clearly Lady Sarah has eyes for no one but Drake.

I have just had the most terrible shock!

I was first to bed this even. Mary Shelton and Lady Sarah were yet to retire to our chamber. As I was about to climb in, I tripped on something bony. It was Ellie's foot! She was curled up under my bed, shivering and shaking and coughing—not at all well!

She explained to me that Mrs. Fadget has taken no notice of her illness and had cruelly insisted she carry on with her duties. She had sent Ellie to bring all the smocks back from the ladies' bedchambers. But having been washing bedlinen all day, Ellie was exhausted, and she'd fallen asleep under my bed. Poor thing! Her skin was burning up and her breath foul, and she kept saying she was wretched cold.

I decided that I would seek out my Uncle Cavendish, the Court Physician—dearly hoping that, as a favour to me, he would tend to Ellie.

Mary Shelton came in just as I was dressing to fetch my uncle.

"Who is that?" she asked. She didn't sound haughty, as most of the other Maids of Honour might do on seeing me nursing Ellie in our chamber. She sounded kind and concerned.

"It's my friend Ellie from the laundry," I

explained. After all, Mary wouldn't have noticed Ellie even if she had seen her about the palace. "She's very sick. And she has no mother to look after her. And Mrs. Fadget, the Deputy Laundress, has been horrible to her!"

Any of the other Maids of Honour might still have fetched Mrs. Champernowne, who would probably have sent Ellie back to the laundry, and I would have been in trouble, no doubt. But Mary didn't. Instead she came and felt Ellie's forehead. "She certainly has a fever," she said. "We must get her out of these wet clothes. They're wringing with sweat. She needs to be tucked up in bed in a clean dry smock. We have to keep her warm, since she has a fever."

I nodded. It was a relief to have someone who knew about these things. I hardly recognized giggly plump Mary Shelton. "How do you know so much?" I asked, very impressed.

Mary shrugged. "I've helped my mother look after our tenants since I was nine years old."

Between us we took off Ellie's worn old kirtle and her dank smock and I got one of my own from the chest and put it on her. Then we tucked her up in my bed, because Mary said Ellie needed a bed with curtains around like mine, to keep her from the bad night airs.

Poor Ellie was too feverish to be quite in her right mind and she looked very worried. "I must go," she fretted. "Mrs. Fadget says I've all the stockings to wring out next—"

"Mrs. Fadget can wait," I said. Well, that isn't quite what I said, but I've made it more respectable for writing down. "You rest, Ellie. We're getting the doctor."

"What? You can't!" she said, trying to sit up. "I can't pay 'im and Mrs. Fadget—"

"It's all right," I told her, getting her to lie down again. "I'm going to fetch my Uncle Cavendish: he won't want paying."

So she sighed and rested her tangled head back down on the pillow. "Never 'ad a doctor before," she muttered. "Not even an apothecary."

But when I got up to fetch my uncle, Ellie would not let go of my hand, so Mary offered to go instead, bless her!

When she came back she had a very disapproving look on her face—rather like Mrs. Champernowne when she catches me writing my daybooke while I'm wearing my white damask. I saw why, and my heart sank a little. My Uncle Cavendish was swaying and staggering behind her. I love my uncle dearly, but he has such a weakness for the drink, and I fear it will be his undoing. Clearly, this even he had drunk far too much wine.

"Lady Graishe, my dear," he said, blinking and swaying over Ellie in my bed, "I'm shorry to shee you ill." He fumbled for her hand.

I was going to tell him it wasn't me, but then I thought he might be embarrassed by his mistake and that might distract him from his doctoring. So I kept quiet and moved behind one of the bed curtains.

He felt Ellie's forehead, his eyes slightly crossed, then her pulses, and then smelled her breath and looked down her throat. "She's got a quinsy," he said to Mary. "Quite sherious. No need to bleed, but she musht have hot drinks every hour and she musht rest and stay warm. Hic. I'll ret—ret—come back in a day or sho." And he staggered out.

Mary was still frowning. But she politely did not refer to my uncle's drunken state. "Poor Ellie," she said. "A quinsy's horrible. My sister had one last year. She said it feels like your throat is full of rusty nails." She patted Ellie's hand. "What you need is a sweet wine posset. I'll make you one."

When it was ready, Mary and I helped Ellie to sit up and sip the hot drink. There was still no sign of Lady Sarah, for which I was grateful, as I was certain she would not take kindly to Ellie's presence. I hoped we could have Ellie safely tucked up in bed and hidden by the curtains before Sarah's arrival.

When Ellie had finished her posset, she gratefully sank back down on the pillows and shut her eyes. Mary went to her bed and I climbed in next to Ellie. It was like having a bread oven in bed next to me—or a furnace even!

Lady Sarah eventually came to bed, waking me up by humming some song about "hauling 'er up-ay-oh." I was so hot then that I had to get out of bed again, so I thought I'd write all this down and cool off at the same time—maybe then I'll be able to sleep.

I woke quite late this morning. Lady Sarah was already risen and gone—off to daydream about Captain Drake, no doubt—and Mary was putting on her white samite gown to attend the Queen. It's a pity really, white looks terrible on her—it quite drains her of colour. She needs pinks and purples to look healthy.

"Grace! At last!" She smiled. "I have a drink here for Ellie—hot water, aqua vitae, honey, and citron. Give her spoonfuls one at a time, because it is hard for her to swallow. I shall be back soon."

Well, of course I was very pleased to do it, so I put on my hunting kirtle and sat spooning the hot drink into Ellie and helping her up to use the close-stool.

There was a soft knock at the door and Masou crept in, just as I was tucking Ellie up in bed again. He looked very nervous—and well he might, because

48

no boys of any kind are supposed to come near the chambers of the Maids of Honour.

"Grace, I can't find Ellie anywhere, and I have looked in every hiding hole in the palace," he whispered. "I don't—"

I moved aside to show him Ellie, softly tucked up.

He sighed with relief. "Allah be praised, I was so full of worry for her," he said. "That hag in the laundry said she neither knew nor cared where Ellie was."

"Ellie has a bad quinsy but Mary and I are looking after her," I told him. "Don't worry, she was seen by my Uncle Cavendish last night and he says she'll be well enough if she stays warm and rests."

Masou nodded, glanced around furtively, and then headed for the door. "I must go now," he said. "Mr. Somers wants all of us who can swim to come to the watersteps and practise a new tumble for the next time the Queen goes to Tilbury by boat."

"Wait a minute, Masou." I stopped him, grabbing a piece of paper. "Will you take a note to that Fadget woman at the laundry?"

Masou bowed. "As my lady pleases."

It always embarrasses me when he does that—which is why he does it, of course. So I wrote a very haughty note to Mrs. Foul Fadget, saying I was unwell and would keep Ellie with me because I required her help, and that she would return soon enough.

Masou trotted off with it after another elaborate bow. Unfortunately, the cushion I threw at him missed and knocked a pot of face cream off Lady Sarah's table.

Mary came back then, carrying some soup from one of the nearer kitchens.

Ellie had been sleeping but she woke up as Mary entered. "Oh no!" she croaked. "Look, the sun's up! Mrs. Fadget will kill me—"

I held her shoulders. "It's all right," I assured her. "I wrote her a note and she can do without you for a bit."

"But I shouldn't ought to be in your bed!" Ellie wailed, looking frightened now. "What will Mrs. Champernowne say?"

Mary grinned cheekily. "Mrs. Champernowne has somehow got the idea that it's Lady Grace who is ill," she said. "And she won't be coming in. Now, sit up and have some soup."

So Ellie struggled up on the pillows and Mary put a napkin round her and fed her the soup. It was a special mess of chicken and dumplings, with a little egg mixed in—Mary has friends in all the kitchens. Perhaps that is why she is so plump.

When she had finished, Mary produced another bowl. "Now this here is a very nasty willow-bark tea," she said. "You have to sip it slowly and let it trickle down your throat to help with the pain. But then you can have a wet sucket to take the taste away," she added.

Suddenly Ellie was crying. "You're both so kind, I don't—"

I put my arms round her and hugged her. "Don't be silly, Ellie, you're sick," I said. "If we were in Whitehall Palace, instead of here at Greenwich with Mrs. Fadget, Mrs. Twiste would put you to bed in the laundry's back room and do just the same as us, now wouldn't she?"

Ellie nodded.

"So, if that foul Fadget woman won't treat you properly, we will," I told her. "And you shall stay right here until you are better."

Afternoon

I have slept most of today, I was so exhausted. I
can't believe all that has happened since last I wrote
in my daybooke! I must begin at the beginning and
try and keep it all straight in my head, because if
ever there was a perfect new case for Her Majesty's
Lady Pursuivant, this is it!

Shortly after I'd finished my last daybooke entry,
Mrs. Champernowne caught me in the corridor.

"I heard you had a quinsy, Lady Grace. I didn't
expect to see you today," she said. "I must say, you
don't look very ill," she observed suspiciously.

"I'm feeling a bit better," I said, trying to make
my face go pale by concentrating.

"Well, in that case," Mrs. Champernowne said
briskly, "I'd be grateful if you would run and find
Lady Sarah for me."

So I did. Only I couldn't find Sarah anywhere.

I went all over Greenwich Palace—even in the stables and the mews—but there was no sign of her. Not in the Withdrawing Chamber, nor the Presence nor the Wardrobe nor the gardens nor the Long Gallery. No sign of Lady Sarah, and no sign of Olwen, either. Eventually, I returned to our chamber to make sure she hadn't skulked back to bed.

Mary was there, knitting a baby's biggin cap, and Ellie was asleep. But no Sarah.

Mary decided to come and help me search. As Ellie was settled, with the bed curtains closed, nobody would know she was there.

As we wandered, we tried to think where else Lady Sarah might be: hidden in an attic, high up in a tree, fallen down a ditch? It made us laugh, but none of these seemed very likely.

We were passing through a courtyard, heading for the Presence Chamber, when a pageboy came over. "Er, you're Maids of Honour, aren't you?" he asked us.

"Yes," I replied cautiously, because sometimes the pageboys try and get you to scream by showing you a spider or something. It doesn't work on me, of course. "Who are you?"

"I'm Robin, my Lady. Do you know Lady Jane Coningsby?" he asked.

"Yes, I do," I told him.

"Well, I've got a message for her from her friend," the pageboy explained.

Lady Jane has a friend? That was a wonder to me. I glanced at Mary and she looked just as surprised. "Go on then, I'll pass it on to her," I offered, keen to know from whom the message came.

"It's from Lady Sarah Bartelmy," said Robin, and he screwed up his eyes in an effort to remember it properly. "She said, 'Please tell my best friend, Lady Jane Coningsby, that I send her my love and she need not worry for me.'"

I stared at him. I'd never heard anything so unlikely in my life. "Lady Sarah said that?" I asked incredulously.

"Yes," Robin replied politely. "Down by the Thames, when the sea captain gave me her letter to deliver."

"The what?" asked Mary.

"The sea captain," Robin repeated. "I don't know his name but I know that's what he was because Lady Sarah called him Captain. He was helping Lady Sarah into his boat, and he called me over and gave me this letter from her, to deliver to Her Majesty."

Mary and I looked at each other, astounded. Lady Sarah, getting into a boat with a sea captain?

"How did you know it was Lady Sarah?" I demanded.

"Everyone knows Lady Sarah Bartelmy," Robin replied. "She's the one with the red hair and the big . . . er . . ."

I nodded hastily. "Now tell us again what happened," I ordered.

The pageboy began to look uncomfortable. "I wasn't doing anything wrong," he insisted truculently. "I'm allowed to fish off the watersteps and I—"

"Not about you, about Lady Sarah," I interrupted impatiently.

"Oh, right," Robin said, looking relieved. "Well, she was being helped into a boat by this sea captain, and he called me over to give me her letter to deliver to the Queen. And as I took the letter, Lady Sarah, she called to me, 'Please tell my best friend, Lady Jane Coningsby, that I send her my love and—'"

"'she need not worry for me,'" I finished for him.

The pageboy nodded vigorously. "Well, if you're

going to pass the message on to Lady Jane, I'd better get this delivered," he said, holding up a letter addressed to Her Majesty the Queen.

I stared at it, then looked at Mary. Her eyes were like saucers.

"Her Majesty will not see you at this hour," Mary said. "She will be dining in her Private Chambers."

Robin sighed and nodded, then went to sit down in a corner of the courtyard and wait.

Mary and I hurried off through a gateway into the next courtyard to discuss what we had discovered.

"Being helped into a boat by a sea captain!" Mary gasped. "Must be Drake—did you *see* them simpering over each other? And sending the Queen a letter . . ." She turned to me. "You know what this might mean, don't you?"

We stopped and stared at each other. I knew Mary had had the same thought as me: "Mayhap she is eloping!" I said.

Mary nodded.

I couldn't help laughing at the thought of elegant Lady Sarah as a sea captain's wife.

Mary was holding her stomach, she was laughing so much. "She'll be climbing up the mast!" she gasped. "She'll be firing a cannon!"

I laughed even harder—but then I suddenly thought of something awful, and stopped laughing. "Lord above," I said. "Think how furious the Queen will be that a Maid of Honour has eloped, to marry without Her permission. She'll send out the Gentlemen of the Guard to capture both of them. Captain Drake will be thrown in the Tower and Lady Sarah will be dragged back in disgrace!"

At that, Mary Shelton stopped laughing, too. It was always fun to watch Lady Sarah getting into trouble with the Queen for squabbling with Lady Jane, or wearing too much face paint, but neither of us wanted to see her get into *real* trouble. Not being-banished-from-Court trouble. Not even Lady Sarah I'm-so-pretty Bartelmy deserved that.

I grabbed Mary's arm. "I have to get a look at that letter!" I told her. Then I turned round and ran back to where Robin was playing knucklebones in the corner of the courtyard. Mary followed.

"Robin," I said, "if you give me that letter, I'll see that Her Majesty gets it. So you can go and get something to eat in the Great Hall rather than waiting around here."

Robin's eyes lit up at the mention of food. He pulled off his cap, bowed—quite gracefully for a nine-year-old—and then put the letter in my hand. "Thank you, my lady," he said quickly, and then sped off in the direction of the Great Hall.

I stared down at the letter, feeling a little sick, because I was now going to commit a sort of treason. After all, you're not supposed to read a message addressed to the Queen before she gets it. But I had to know what Lady Sarah said in her letter. And anyway, I reasoned, Her Majesty's clerks read most of her letters for her—she gets so many she would never have time to read them all.

"Come on!" I whispered to Mary, and hurried off towards our bedchamber, with Mary puffing along behind.

As soon as we were in our bedchamber, I blocked the door with a stool and lit one of the candles. Then I got the penknife out of my penner and heated up the blade in the candle's flame. One of the clerks showed me once how to open a letter without breaking the seal—so that you can read it and seal it up again, and no one the wiser! If this letter turned out to be boring Court business, I intended to do just that, and then take it to the Queen. Holding my breath, I put the letter on the table and used the hot knife blade to gently ease the seal off the paper. I unfolded the letter. It said:

Palace of Placentia, Greenwich
The seventh day of May, in the Year of Our Lord 1569

Your Most Gracious Majesty,
I must tell you that I am ardently in love with Captain Drake. We are going aboard his ship, whereupon his chaplain shall marry us and so I shall be his wife for ever. I have taken Olwen with me.

Your humble servant,
Sarah, Lady Bartelmy

I could feel a breeze in my mouth, so I shut my jaw.

Mary, who had been squeaking about how I mustn't open the Queen's letter, peered over my shoulder and read it, too. "So! It is confirmed!" she gasped.

"What's 'appening?" asked a croaky voice from my bed. "What are you doing, Grace?"

"It seems Lady Sarah has eloped with Captain Drake," I told Ellie.

Ellie was silent for a moment. "Cor!" she said reverently.

I was thinking as hard as I possibly could, as hard as a Lady Pursuivant, trying to make sense of it all. Lady Sarah had shamelessly flirted with

Captain Drake, and he'd promised her presents, but was she *really* stupid enough to run away with a piratical sea captain? She would be banished from Court for a certainty, and she loves it here. Even I had to admit it was hard to believe she would act so foolishly. And yet, I had the evidence of her letter in my hand.

"What do you think the Queen will do to her?" Ellie asked ghoulishly. "Put her in the stocks? Flog her?"

"She'll be in the most terrible disgrace," said Mary seriously.

"Oh, is that all?" Ellie sounded quite disappointed.

I stood up and went over to Lady Sarah's corner of the chamber. Her jewellery casket and her ivory comb and the cochineal-pink wax she uses on her lips to make them shine were all still sitting on her dressing table. So was the smelly stuff made of crushed woodlice that she puts on her spots, and the bit of unwashed white lamb's wool she rubs her hands with to keep them soft. It just didn't make sense. "Look," I said, "she's left all her toilette behind—how will she comb her hair and cure her spots? She's even left her jewellery."

"Now that *is* odd," agreed Ellie. "I never 'eard of

anyone eloped what didn't take all the jewellery she could lay her hands on."

"I truly think she has taken leave of her senses," said Mary, shaking her head in bafflement. "What with the elopement, and that extraordinary message, sending her love to her best friend, Lady Jane! I believe she'd be more likely to send her love to that old crone Mrs. Champernowne, for the Lord's sake!"

I nodded. "You're right, Mary," I agreed. "Anyone who knows Lady Sarah would see the untruth of her message to Lady Jane." Then a thought came into my head. "But what if that was Sarah's intention?" I said slowly. "What if she was trying to alert those who know her that all is not as it seems?" I held up the letter. "Mayhap *this* is untrue, too?"

I rushed over to the window and held Sarah's letter to the Queen up to the light, to examine it more closely. Was it really Sarah's writing? "I'm not sure this is Lady Sarah's hand," I muttered as I studied the letters.

"But how can you tell?" asked Ellie, who was sitting up now, still quite flushed, but determined not to be left out even though she cannot read. "Aren't you all taught to write the same?"

"Let me see," said Mary.

I went and sat on the bed along with Mary, so that we could all see. It is true that we have all been strictly schooled in writing—and thus our letters look very alike. But Sarah's hand has one special characteristic. "Look," I said. "This letter *appears* to be from Lady Sarah, but Sarah always pens a big curly tail on her *ys*—I think she learned it deliberately, to be like the Queen."

"Oh yes," agreed Mary. "I once sat next to her when she was writing to her father complaining, as usual, that she had nothing new to wear. She took ages over her curly *ys*—I grew quite bored watching her."

I passed no comment on Mary's nosiness, as I was too excited by my discovery. "Yes: see these words, *Majesty* and *marry* and *Bartelmy*?" I said, pointing them out to Mary and Ellie. "The *ys* don't have curly tails at all. I don't think this letter *is* from Lady Sarah. I think it's a *forgery*! And that means Drake has taken Lady Sarah away against her will!"

"Cor!" breathed Ellie again.

Mary was speechless.

I paced up and down the room. "Think about it," I told them, while they both goggled at me. "Lady Sarah was flirting with Captain Drake. Maybe he misunderstood—he isn't entirely familiar with the ways of Court, after all. She won't agree to marry him, so he captures her and takes her to his ship. He's a pirate, he's used to doing dangerous things. Then, when they're well out to sea, his chaplain will marry them and the thing is done!"

Mary nodded. "It happens sometimes," she agreed. "A cousin of mine was taken by her wicked stepfather to wed his nephew. Luckily, my father, together with some other gentlemen, rode after them and saved her just in time. Once you're married, there's nothing to be done—and your husband gets all your wealth!" Mary tutted sadly, then picked up an empty wine flagon. "It's time for your next posset, Ellie," she said. "I'll be back soon." And she slipped out of the room.

How dare Captain Drake think he could abduct one of us just because he felt like it! I was so angry, it made me want to rescue Lady Sarah—even if she is the worst possible chamber-mate and does insist on using foul, smelly spot creams.

"If I tell the Queen what's happened and explain that the letter is forged, perchance the Queen will let me go and investigate and rescue Lady Sarah," I said hopefully to Ellie. "If I go down to Tilbury right away, they might not have sailed yet and I could get her back quietly."

"Don't be a Bedlamite," replied Ellie. "The Queen would never let you do that!"

"She said I was her Lady Pursuivant and I could investigate mysteries at the palace," I reminded her, feeling quite annoyed. But I knew Ellie was probably right.

Ellie shook her head, then winced. "Her Majesty might let you 'vestigate within the Verge of Court, but she'll never let you go gallivanting off down to Tilbury docks," she declared. "She'll send men, lots of them, with halberds and swords. Hey! Do you think there'll be a fight? D'you think Drake's sailors will fight them off?" Ellie started coughing again in her excitement.

"Doubtless," I agreed. It was exciting to think of the battle, but my heart was sinking like a stone as I thought of what it would mean. "But if there is any such brawl and Lady Sarah is brought back by the Queen's Gentlemen of the Guard, everyone in the Court will know of it," I pointed out to Ellie. "The gossip will be all over London in half a day, the ballad-sellers will be singing of it by dinner time! Lady Sarah's reputation will be ruined, whatever really happened—and whether she was willing *or* forced. She will have to leave Court like Katharine Broke, and her father might even disinherit her. Then she'll have to marry a barrister or somebody awful like that!"

"Well, there's nothing you can do about it," Ellie declared. "So you'll have to seal up the letter again and give it to the Queen."

I almost agreed, but then I was struck by another idea—it was the beginning of a plan, but a plan so bold that I hardly dared mention it. If I hadn't been so angry with Captain Drake I don't suppose I ever would have thought of it, but, "There *is* something I can do about it, Ellie," I said slowly, clenching my fist on the forged letter. "I can go to Tilbury *secretly*, and try to rescue Lady Sarah with no one being any the wiser. If I succeed, her reputation will not be ruined and she will not be sent from Court!"

Ellie just stared at me with her mouth open.

And I stood there, trying to look brave and determined—which I think was very noble of me considering what a nuisance Lady Sarah is!

At that moment Mary Shelton came back with the posset and I told her my intention straight away, before I had time to change my mind—because I knew I would be taking a very great risk; only my outrage at Drake's behaviour made me determined.

It took another half-hour of arguing, but in the

end neither Mary nor Ellie could think of any better way to help Sarah—unless you count sitting on our bums and wringing our hands. So we came up with a plan so that I could slip away to Tilbury: Mary would tell everyone that I had suffered a relapse, and that Lady Sarah was now ill in bed, too. She would pretend she was looking after both of us. That way, no one would come near, in case it was something infectious, and Ellie could continue to be looked after in my bed. "And I think Lady Sarah took Olwen with her. So we'd better include her, too," I added.

Mary giggled. "So now I have four patients, one visible and three invisible. Don't you think your uncle, Dr. Cavendish, will wonder . . . ?"

"My uncle won't even notice," I assured her.

Mary shook her head. "I'm not sure if you are very brave or very stupid," she said with feeling. "You don't even *like* Lady Sarah."

That is true. But I believed that Lady Sarah had already suffered the indignity of abduction, and as Lady Pursuivant I intended to do my best to see that she should not also suffer the injustice of disgrace because of it. Not even Sarah—though she is most trying—deserves that.

I made sure I had some money with me and considered taking my daybooke—only it is too precious and I would not want it to get spoiled at the docks. Tilbury is a damp and untidy place, so I resolved to leave my daybooke in my chamber but to take careful note of my adventure for writing up later.

Of course, I needed the right clothes for my mission. So I hurried down to the buttery, where Masou and the other acrobats often go after a hard practice to drink mild ale and boast.

Sure enough, Masou was there. I dragged him into an alcove and told him what had happened. His eyes nearly popped out of his head.

"Allah, forgive me!" he cried. "I saw them getting into the boat myself. It was rowed by some ugly-looking ogres—and the Captain lifted my Lady Sarah and carried her on board when she didn't get in by herself. But I was busy practising a juggle and balance and I never thought anything of it, so, alas, I raised no alarm!"

"That must have been Captain Drake!" I exclaimed, then patted Masou's arm reassuringly because he looked so horrified. "Can you tell me anything else?" I asked.

"The lady was as stiff and white as paper—perhaps the Captain held her under an enchantment—" he mused.

"Masou!" I said. "This isn't the time for your romantic nonsense!"

He looked embarrassed. "I heard her asking him about Olwen and whether she was safe," he remembered.

Aha! I thought. That explains why Sarah didn't struggle or call out directly for help when Drake was putting her into the boat. He used Olwen's well-being as ransom. What a cowardly bully.

As quickly as I could I told Masou what I was going to do. "But I shall need to go in disguise—as a boy—if I am not to attract attention," I explained. "So I shall need a boy's clothes. Is there anyone's I could borrow?"

Masou thought a bit, then his eyes lit up and he nodded. "French Louis's son has a new outfit, and he is a beanplant like you. We should find his old apparel in the tiring chamber."

We crept off to where the acrobats change before a performance, a little room off the Great Hall. The clothes were old and worn and quite smelly, but I nipped into a closet, took off my kirtle and smock, and put on the shirt and hose. I came out pulling on the doublet and leather jerkin, then I put my eating knife on the belt. I thought I looked very well indeed.

But Masou sighed as he looked at me, and then he

brought out a pair of shears. I flinched and he tut-ted. "Did you ever see a boy with locks as long as yours?" he asked.

I flushed. He was right, of course, but—cut my hair? I wasn't sure if I dared. Mrs. Champernowne would have a fit if she found out—several fits!

"Come, it will grow again," Masou reassured me, and without more ado he cut it all to one short length.

I couldn't believe it was all gone—just like that! It felt very peculiar indeed, but as my mousy brown hair was hardly my crowning glory, I found I didn't mind so much. And I could always use a hairpiece to hide the damage later, I thought.

Masou then found me a blue woollen cap, helped me to put it on the right way, and showed me my reflection in the big mirror with the crack in it that the acrobats use.

I gasped. With my short hair and my flat-as-a-pancake chest (*when* will I start growing outwards as well as up?) I made a very believable boy. Not far off handsome, in fact. I did a bow—not very good.

Masou sighed. Then he took down two cloaks from a rail. "I am coming with you," he announced.

"But Mr. Somers might beat you if he finds out!" I argued. "You don't have to come."

"Of course I do," snorted Masou. "What do you know of being a boy? Nothing. And if *you* are found out, there will be a most dreadful scandal." He shook his head. "Walk over there."

I did and he sighed again. "Stride, swagger!" he instructed. "Don't smile. And stare straight at people."

I walked up and down trying to swagger. It felt very odd to have so much air around my legs, and yet cloth chafing between.

"Not bad," Masou admitted. "When you talk to anyone, remember to say 'sir' or you'll be buffeted."

I heard the clock chime one, and worried that Drake might soon have readied his ship to go to sea. "Come on, Masou," I urged, "we must hurry!"

We flitted through the back passages of Greenwich, past the bakery and the dairy and the little laundry—where Mrs. Fadget was screaming at some very tired-looking laundrywomen—and down to the kitchen steps.

Masou shouted, "Oars! Oars!"

At last a boat drew up and I looked nervously at it, waiting for the waterman to help me board.

"What are you waiting for?" Masou dug me with his elbow. "Jump in!"

Of course, boys don't get helped, so I gulped and jumped and managed to keep my balance. In fact, it was easier because I hadn't any petticoats or stays.

Masou followed me, stepping aboard lightly.

"Tilbury," I said to the man. "And as fast as you can."

"Won't make no difference," said the waterman. "Tide's still against us."

"But it's an urgent message for Captain Drake from the Queen," I told him desperately.

"You'd better help row then, lad," the waterman replied bluntly.

Masou showed me the spare pair of oars and fitted them in the little metal things on either side of the boat. He took one himself and started dipping it into the water. I tried to copy him but the oar kept popping out when I wasn't expecting it and making me fall backwards. It was very annoying and frustrating, and made the waterman laugh and shake his head.

"Clumsy, ain't you?" he remarked.

It seemed to take ages to get to Tilbury and I was puffing long before then.

"What's wrong with your mate?" grunted the waterman to Masou. "He sick, then?"

"No, he's just outgrown his strength," replied Masou with a grin. "Look what a beanpole he is."

"Humph," was all I could manage.

We rowed and rowed and at last we came to the Tilbury watersteps. They must have tidied up for the Queen for it looked messier than I remembered it, and even more muddy. I paid the waterman, and then Masou made me go behind some barrels and arrange my purse in my crotch! Under my codpiece! He said I had to or it would be stolen the first time I blinked. He turned away while I did it and I heard spattering.

"You'd best go, too," he said, gesturing.

And that was when I realized what was going to be the biggest problem of all: how on earth could I make water? It's never a problem usually: either there's a chamber pot to use or, if we are on progress or out hunting, I just find a quiet grassy spot and my farthingale hides me. But now I wore hose, and a codpiece between my legs that unlaced at the front—only that wouldn't do *me* any good!

"Um . . . Masou . . . ," I said, wondering if Lady Sarah was worth this humiliation, "um . . . how . . . ?"

"Undo all the laces except the back ones and then squat," Masou instructed. "And try and do it where nobody sees." He shook his head and tutted.

So I did just that behind a big barrel—and found it very strange and draughty.

As we hurried along the docks, Masou tried to teach me to whistle. I had never realized there were so many things you had to know to be a boy.

"And by the way," he asked, "what is your name going to be?"

Another thing I hadn't thought of. I could hardly go around calling myself Lady Grace in doublet and hose. "Um . . . Gregory? It's a bit like Grace," I suggested.

"Right, *Gregory*, please tell me you have a plan," said Masou. He was sounding a bit nervous now.

"Of course I have a plan," I blustered. "We go aboard Captain Drake's ship, find Lady Sarah, and get her off before it sails. Simple! But we don't want to meet Captain Drake, because I'm sure he'll recognize me and then who knows what he'll do?"

"If he's rogue enough to kidnap Lady Sarah," Masou pointed out, "you could end up married to the First Mate or something!"

"Well, we're not going to see him, and we're not going to get caught," I told Masou firmly, feeling a bit annoyed. Now he'd made *me* nervous too!

We passed a ship that was being built in the dry dock. It was swarming with people, full of the sounds of sawing and hammering and shouts. Then we passed the big square pond where we had raced the two model ships. The winches were still there, now being perched upon by seagulls.

We asked everybody we met which was Captain Drake's ship. One person said it was about to sail. So we rushed to the quayside where he'd pointed. The sailors were in the rigging and there were ropes everywhere, along with the sound of creaking and stamping and a song that sounded like "Oo-ay and up she rises, oo-ay and up she rises . . ."

I was in a panic to get aboard and rushed up to the pigtailed sailor standing by the gangplank. "We've got a message for Captain Drake!" I gasped, forgetting to be nervous. "Let us on the ship!"

"No," said the sailor. He gave me and Masou a knowing grin.

"Why not? We've got to talk to the Captain!" I insisted.

"Well, you won't find him on this ship," the sailor said. "This 'ere is the *Silver Arrow*—Hugh Derby, Captain. If you want Captain Drake you need to go to the *Judith* over there." He pointed at the other two-masted ship in the next quay.

Masou and I hastily stepped back from the gangplank, as the sailors hauled up the anchor. The *Silver Arrow* started moving away from the quay. She was being pulled by ropes attached to smaller rowing boats. There were lots of shouts as one sailor removed the mooring ropes from the big tree trunks at the quayside and then leaped lightly across the gap onto the ship.

"Derby's in a hurry," commented a sailor behind us, as he watched the *Silver Arrow* move slowly out into the river. "Where's he off to? I wonder. He's too early for the ebb."

Masou and I shrugged at him, then hurried towards the *Judith*.

We found Drake's ship still moored to the quay, with sailors swarming round it. Baskets and nets full of loaves of bread were being loaded into the hold, and a boy was handing a package to the sailor guarding the gangplank.

"Package for Captain Drake," he said.

The sailor took it and nodded. "I'll see that 'e gets it," he replied.

The boy left and Masou swaggered up to take his place. I followed, doing my best to swagger as well. "Captain aboard?" Masou asked the sailor.

"Aye, but he's below."

Below what? I wondered, but didn't ask. I just stood there trying to look, well—boyish.

"We got a message for him," said Masou.

"I'll give it to 'im," said the sailor.

"We've been told to give it to him personally," Masou countered.

"Ah, now would you be the boys sent from the steelyard?" the sailor asked.

"Might be," said Masou, using the opening the sailor had unwittingly given him.

"In that case, you can come aboard and wait in the Great Cabin for him—but mind, no tricks now. Captain's got a short way with lads what annoy him." The sailor made a throat-slitting motion and grinned.

Masou salaamed, and I pulled at my cap as I've seen the kitchen boys do, then we made our way up the gangplank. I swaggered for all I was worth—and nearly fell off.

"Tell your mate to sober up afore he talks to the Captain!" the sailor shouted at Masou.

Masou looked at me sidelong. I could tell that he was trying not to laugh. "Less sideways, more forwards," he directed.

"This is so difficult," I complained, puffing.

"Compared with petticoats?" Masou asked. He did have a point.

We picked our way across the deck between baskets waiting to be stowed and net bags full of cannonballs and barrels. Masou told me that the Great Cabin was located in the sterncastle, at the blunt end of the ship.

I had to duck my head as I passed through a low door into the small room that was called the Great Cabin. I stared around, at the table covered with maps and papers, and the cot in one corner. A sword and a pistol in its case were hung on one wall. The others had half-finished paintings on them; they were quite clumsy, showing what appeared to be a lot of people standing on big round balls and looking out to sea. The solitary window looked out on sailors hammering on the deck. But there was no sign of Lady Sarah. And I had been so sure she would be there!

I crept into the next cabin, which had two cots in it, and the next, which had three cots and three small chests. I couldn't believe Sarah wasn't in any of them. Where had he put her?

"Any luck?" Masou whispered to me, from where he was keeping watch at the half-open door.

"No!" I whispered back.

Our hearts beating like mad, we climbed down a ladder to look in the tiny cabins below. But we didn't find her anywhere. And there was so much more ship to search than I'd expected.

Eventually, Masou shook his head. The sun was starting to go down. "Come on," he said. "She's not here—we'll have to leave."

"But we haven't even been into the front half of the ship," I pointed out. "We at least ought to look."

We crept like mice along the low space under the main deck, where the crew's bedrolls were tucked alongside the guns. A little further along we passed a little eating room for the officers, where tables hung from the ceiling. The big sullen-looking boy, who had kept the seagulls away from the feast when we visited the docks with the Queen, was listlessly scrubbing at them. Luckily, he was too busy muttering about the First Mate to notice us.

Then Masou found a ladder that went right down into the belly of the ship. Down here the darkness was full of barrels and hams hanging on beams. It looked like the dirtiest, smokiest kitchen you ever saw—and the smell was awful.

We crept past the barrels and found a fire burning in a brick grate, with a huge copper full of water above it. Benches and stools were set around it as if it were an inn. Masou poked a basket that had loaves of bread in it and I had a sniff at an open barrel where some salt beef seemed to be soaking.

"Oi! You two! What are you doing down here?" A skinny man in a dirty apron jumped down from a ladder. He had a sack over his shoulder. "Get out of it! Stealing food—I'll 'ave you!" He dropped the sack and started throwing potatoes at us, so Masou and I ran away as fast as we could. Once we had escaped, I gasped indignantly, "Stealing food! That horrible stuff? Why would anyone want to?"

Masou just shook his head and laughed.

We searched on until we reached the pointed front end of the ship, where we found a triangular room filled with folded sails, all marked with chalk symbols. I noticed a bowl on the floor—and then something moved slightly in the shadows. I peered into the darkness and saw a long, curvy shape. My heart leaped with excitement. It had to be Lady Sarah with those famous curves of hers! "She's here!" I gasped.

Shocked that she'd been tied up there in the dark,

I rushed over to release her. Masou followed, and together we pushed past the huge packages of sails to reach Lady Sarah . . .

Only it wasn't. It was just a sail, tied up so it looked like someone rather busty lying down. The movement I'd seen was a little family of cats—a mother and her kittens, nestling in the folds. The mother cat meowed at me and then gave a warning hiss.

"Ahh," I said. I couldn't help it. The kittens were adorable with their huge eyes and little paws. "It's all right, I won't harm—"

"Is she there?" Masou nudged me from behind.

"No," I said. "It's kittens. I don't know what we—"

"Shhh!" Masou whispered fiercely, staring over his shoulder.

There were voices outside the door. One of them was Captain Drake's! I dived behind the sail with the cats in it, and Masou shrank into the space behind the door.

Captain Drake's lively face appeared round the door as he peered into the dim room. "You've rousted the sails out well?" he demanded.

"Aye, Captain," said a voice behind him. "We shook 'em out and checked 'em for holes yesterday, while you were at Court."

No, you didn't, I thought, while my heart went *boom-da-da-boom*. That family of cats looks far too cosy to have been disturbed for a week. I prayed none of the cats would move and attract Captain Drake's attention. *Where have you put Lady Sarah, you evil man?* I thought, staring at him. *She must be here somewhere.*

"Very good," said Drake. And then he pulled the door shut.

As Masou and I hid there in the shadows, we heard bolts slide home on the outside of the door! We stared at each other in horror as the footsteps moved away. Then Masou began muttering to himself in his own language and pushing at the door.

I felt my way over to him, my mouth totally dry. We tried everything to slide the bolts open from the wrong side. Masou jiggled with his knife, I worked on the hinges—but to no avail.

"If only it was locked, I could pick it," Masou said, thumping his fist on the door in frustration.

"Shhh," I warned. "Don't do that, someone will hear and we'll be in terrible trouble."

"I hate it!" he panted. "I hate being locked in, I . . ." He slipped back into Arabic again.

I felt for his shoulder and patted it. "Masou," I

81

said, "they'll have to come and get sails sooner or later, and then they'll let us out."

"No, I have to get out now!" he insisted. He banged with his fists and shouted at the top of his voice—but he was drowned out by a sudden tramping of feet above us. A work song began: "Oo-ay and up she rises, oo-ay and up she rises . . ." The feet settled to a steady stamp and heave, and there was a creaking and clattering and a long squealing sound.

"What's that, Masou?" I caught his hands to stop them drumming. "Listen, what is it?"

He was quiet for a long time. "I think it's the capstan for the anchor," he said eventually.

"Eh?" He was talking Sailorish.

"They're pulling up the anchor," Masou clarified.

"Oh," I said. "Um . . . does that mean they're getting ready to sail?"

Masou nodded, and then he started banging again. Except nobody heard because of all the noise from the anchor.

Masou was panting heavily by now, so I took hold of his hands again and patted them. It was very frightening being locked up in the dark, and knowing that the ship was getting ready to sail soon. But trying to calm Masou helped me not to feel so frightened myself. I'd never known him be so scared before—I'd seen him juggle with fire while balancing on top of a little pole, and not so much as blink. I had been the one with my heart in my mouth then. And seeing him frightened now made me feel guilty for bringing him on such a mad escapade. We had found no trace of either Lady Sarah or Olwen anywhere.

There were thuds and bangs and shouts. The ship began to rock in a different way. There was more creaking, the sound of counting, and men shouting, "Heave!" And then two big splashes. More shouting. The ship was definitely moving—it seemed to find a new way to rock every minute.

I had thought it would be simple to rescue Lady Sarah, but now we needed rescuing ourselves! What if they didn't need sails for days and days? What if they were going to the Azores or New Spain? What if the ship got caught in a storm and sank? What if it went into battle with the Spanish? I felt horribly sick with panic, but I forced myself to keep quiet for fear of making Masou any worse.

I don't know how long I sat there in the dark, listening to the happy squeaks of the kittens with their mother, and worrying about what would happen to us. Masou calmed down a bit after a while—I could hear him breathing more steadily. The ship was rolling from side to side, which was making me feel peculiar. I tried to take my mind off it by thinking about Lady Sarah—what if Drake's regard for her had been nothing but an act and he wanted her only for her wealth? Or what if he had lost patience with her—which, heaven knows, is easy to do—and had put her in irons in the brig, with the rats? She'd be so frightened. She didn't even like *mice* and she was so silly and timid. . . .

After what felt like a very long time, there was another kind of movement—like a horse makes when it canters. It was quite soothing, really. Although I was so frightened and worried (*what* would the Queen do when I got back—*if* I got back?), the motion was comforting and I curled up on one of the sails and dozed off.

The next thing I knew there was a bright light! A loud bang! A rough man's voice calling, "Tom?" in the distance. Then the man's voice shouted, "What the—! God's teeth, what's this? What the hell are you two boys doing here?"

I was thick-headed with sleep, trying to work

out how a man with a big gold earring and a pigtail had got into the bedchamber of the Maids of
Honour. . . .

Masou scrambled to his feet, looking terrified.

The man called over his shoulder, "Mr. Price,
we'm got stowaways again, bloody little rats." Then
he turned back to Masou and me. "Come on, you!
Out of there—and you'd better not've damaged any
of they sails, you hear?"

He not only had a pigtail, he was as wide as a barrel and one of his front teeth was missing. He
grabbed hold of Masou by the arm and slung him
out into the passage, where Masou rolled neatly and
came to his feet. Then he strode towards me,
grabbed my jerkin, and did the same to me. I landed
in a heap.

"Why did you do that?" I shouted, climbing to my
feet again, outraged at his unfairness. "It's not our
fault, we got locked in!"

The man swung his arm and hit me so hard round
the head that I fell over again, my head ringing and
my ear burning. I felt too dizzy to get up for a bit.
Masou came and stood between me and the man.

"What were you doing in there at all? Looking for
vittles to steal, I'll be bound!" shouted the man.

"No, sir, we weren't," replied Masou. "We were lost."

I was very impressed at how steady his voice was.

"Call me a liar, would ye?" roared the man, and he aimed a clip round Masou's ear too—except Masou was clever enough to duck and roll so he didn't get hit.

I struggled to my knees and then decided it might be sensible to stay on the floor. "It's true," I said. "We were *lost*." But I could hardly tell him that we'd become lost while looking for the girl his Captain had kidnapped, now could I?

"A likely story!" He kicked at Masou and then at me. "Up! Get up and explain yourselves to the Mate."

At least he wasn't taking us to the Captain—yet. I rubbed the bruise on my bum where I'd landed on the floor, and my swollen ear, then scurried up the ladder after Masou.

As we got to the top, Masou muttered to me, "Shut up and let me talk. I don't want you making him so angry he throws us overboard."

"He wouldn't dare—" I began.

"Who'd know?" Masou pointed out. "You're not important now, *Gregory*, so be quiet!"

I realized with a chill that Masou was right! I was no longer Lady Grace Cavendish, with the protection of Her Majesty the Queen. I was Gregory, suspected stowaway! I could see that Masou was frightened—a different sort of frightened from when we were shut in—and it was making him fierce. I started to get frightened, too. This wasn't at all what I'd planned. We were supposed to be back at Court with Lady Sarah, safe and sound, by now!

We went up another ladder and found ourselves in the middle of the deck, next to the biggest mast. There was a strong wind blowing, and big waves, and no land anywhere around. When I looked up I could see lots of sails billowing in the wind, and ropes everywhere, all crossing each other.

The wide man who'd found us gripped us both by the shoulder and shoved us forwards, until we were standing in front of another broad man in a woollen doublet and a ruff. His hands tightened and he shoved us again so we both fell on our knees.

"Stowaways, Mr. Newman, sir," he said. "Found 'em in the sail locker."

Mr. Newman looked down at us as if we were dead rats, and sighed. "Have either of you sailed before?" he asked.

"Yes, sir," answered Masou quickly, "I have. A two-master out of Dunkirk when I was younger." I remembered Masou telling me that he'd only been six years old at the time, but I didn't think he'd want me to mention that. "I'm an acrobat now," he added. "My name is Masou—and this is my mate, Gregory."

Mr. Newman looked a bit more interested. "Acrobat, eh? Can you climb?" he asked Masou.

"Yes, and I can tumble, sir," Masou told him proudly.

"Go on then," said Mr. Newman, folding his arms.

Masou bowed, stood on tiptoe, then bounced—turned a neat somersault in the air—and came back down lightly on his feet.

"And you?" said Mr. Newman to me.

"Um, please, Mr. Newman, where's the ship going?"

He scowled. "None of your business, boy. That's up to the Captain. Now, have you sailed before?"

"Er . . . no, I haven't sailed," I said, then, as he frowned, remembered to add, "sir."

"So what can you do?" Mr. Newman enquired.

"Um, I can . . . I . . ." I thought desperately for something. "I can embroider, sir . . . I was apprenticed to the Queen's Wardrobe, but I ran away because it was boring. And . . . I . . . can paint and draw, too," I added, hoping that the patterns I'd designed for my embroideries would stand me in good stead.

"Soft as a girl, in other words," said Mr. Newman disgustedly. "You, Masou, are you afraid of heights?"

"No, sir, not at all," Masou replied.

"Good," Mr. Newman said. "The banner's snagged at the topsail yard. You and your mate go up there and free it." He pointed up and up and up the mast that was nearest the front of the ship, to where there was a sort of lump tangled in the ropes.

Masou knuckled his forehead. "Yes, sir." He went over to the rail and climbed on it.

I stared in horror at the enormous mast stretching upwards into the sky. "What if we fall?" I quavered.

"You'll die," said the man who had found us. "And that'd be an easy way out."

"You can do as you're told, boy," added Mr. Newman, "or you can go in the brig. But you get no food if you don't work. Up you go."

Well, it was long past breakfast time and I was thirsty, too, so I gulped and nodded.

Mr. Newman frowned. "I don't like your manners, Gregory," he said. "Mend 'em or you'll be in worse trouble than you can imagine."

"Y-yes, sir," I replied, and went to follow Masou.

He hadn't started climbing yet. "You go first," he whispered to me. "Then if you slip, I can catch you. Just think of it as a tree," he suggested.

"Hell's teeth!" I exclaimed nervously. I don't mind climbing trees, but this was a tree that was rocking back and forth with the waves.

"Wait for the ship to roll the other way," instructed Masou. "Now, up . . ."

I climbed, holding on as tight as I could. My knees were knocking, but at least I could hear Masou behind me. We went up and up, past the huge yellow-white sheets of the sails and about a thousand ropes. But the ladder—what was it Captain Drake had called them? Ratlines? Anyway, the rungs got narrower and narrower and then stopped under the platform, halfway up the mast, that he'd called the fighting top.

"Now what?" I wailed. "There's no more ladder!"

"See the ropes going out to the edge of the fighting top?" called Masou from below me.

I looked, and saw ratlines I hadn't noticed, stretching from the mast out to the edge of the top—

but what good were they? I'd be hanging right out over the deck, which was really far below us now. "Yes," I whispered, knowing what Masou was going to say.

He did. "We have to climb them."

"What?" I squealed, sounding almost as squeaky as Lady Sarah when she's seen a mouse. "I can't!"

"Yes, you can," Masou said firmly.

"But . . . it's too high . . . I'll be hanging by my hands. I can't, Masou!" I pleaded.

"Yes, you can!" shouted Masou fiercely. "You *can* do it, because you *have* to!"

Masou had never spoken to me like that before. Nobody had. But I still could not move.

"Allah save us," he muttered. "Grace, I cannot coax you, there's no time. You've climbed harder things; I know you can do this, but the only way for you to know it too is to try. Now *climb* the *tree*! Or else you will have to go back down and confess that you're a girl."

Suddenly I felt furious with myself. Who was acting like Lady Sarah now? Masou was right. I would *not* give up and admit to being a girl just because I was scared of climbing the ratlines.

Heart hammering, I put my hand up, gripped one rung of the rope ladder, then the other, got my toes into a narrow gap, then my other foot . . . I was leaning right out, with nothing under me for miles and miles . . . If I fell, I'd die! Toes clawing round the rung of the ladder, I reached up for the next rung, then the next. The edge of the top was the worst, I had to hold on with one hand, move the other over the edge to the new set of ratlines there, then wrap my arm around it, then reach over with the other hand . . .

Suddenly Masou was there, hauling me up onto the top by my jerkin. He must have whisked up on the other side of the mast. "Well done," he whispered in my ear. "You see? You did it!"

I lay there for a minute, gasping and shaking, and then got slowly to my feet.

Masou pointed to the next, narrower set of ratlines, which went right up to the point of the mast where the cloth was tangled in a rope.

"Oh no," I gasped, my heart thundering enough to crack my chest.

Masou grinned encouragingly at me and began to climb.

I didn't want to be left alone on the high tossing little platform. So I started following him.

He looked down at me and shook his head. "Not this one. The other side."

So I climbed down, edged over to the other set of ratlines, and started climbing again.

When I caught Masou up at the highest place on the mast, he was already struggling with the cloth bunched in the ropes. I wrapped one leg around the ratlines and tugged at the tangle. Then I stopped and looked more closely. It was pulled up too tight. I could see we'd never get it free like that. "Loosen it!" I yelled down to the deck, as loud as I could.

There was a movement down there, which I could hardly see for all the sails in the way. The ropes moved past each other a couple of times, and then I could see the bit that was caught and tease it out with my fingers.

Suddenly the banner flapped and took the wind and floated out above the ship.

Masou grinned at me. "See, my lady? You did it."

I smiled back, trying not to think about getting down. "You should call me Gregory," I reminded him.

Masou scampered back down to the fighting top like a monkey. He waited for me there as I edged my way much more carefully, trying not to look down.

When I reached him, he showed me how to slide my feet out over the edge of the fighting top, catch my toes in the rungs and then let myself down onto the main ratlines.

Then he grabbed a rope. "Now don't try to get down this way," he warned me with a mischievous gleam in his eyes. Next thing I knew, he was sliding down the rope, hand over hand, all the way down to the deck!

I climbed my way down the ratlines—but much more quickly than before, because I was so relieved to be going down, not up.

Masou flourished a bow at Mr. Newman when we landed back on the deck. I copied him.

"Hm," Mr. Newman said, looking at Masou with some respect. "You've not been a ship's boy before?"

"No, sir," Masou answered.

"You might make a very fine topman with care," Mr. Newman decided. Then he turned to me. "You, Gregory, I don't know what use you might be. Did you say you could paint?"

"Yes, sir," I lied.

"Good. Go and report to the Boatswain. In fact, both of you go," Mr. Newman ordered.

I wondered if we were going to get any dinner. My stomach was grumbling. But I didn't think it would be a good plan to ask. So I went the way he pointed and found a harassed-looking white-haired man carrying some clay pots towards the Great Cabin—the last place I wanted to go, in case the Captain saw me. I heard Masou groan behind me.

"Sir, sir, are you the Boatswain?" I asked.

"Aye. Ah yes, Mr. Newman said you claimed to be a painter and stainer," the Boatswain declared.

"Only a 'prentice, sir," I hedged quickly.

"No matter. Come this way," he said, and led us into the Great Cabin.

I followed, with my shoulders hunched. Captain Drake wasn't there, thank goodness. "Where's the Captain?" I asked.

"He's training some new gunners," the Boatswain replied. "Now then. See here, this painting needs finishing." It was the scrawl of people standing on balls looking at waves. "This is to show the Queen when she came to Tilbury."

Aha! They weren't balls, they were kirtles. I nodded and tried not to smile at how crude the picture was.

"There's the paint," said the Boatswain. "And there's the picture. Get to it." And he left us to it.

"Are you angry with me for ordering you about up there?" Masou asked me, once the Boatswain was out of earshot.

I smiled at him. "No, it helped. How did you know what to say?"

He flashed his white teeth in a grin. "It's how Mr. Somers talks to me if I think I cannot do a tumble he wants."

I looked at the paints. There were some good colours—a red and a blue and a yellow and a black and a white. I took one of the brushes—which were far too thick—and gave it to Masou, then started to improve the kirtles of the Ladies-in-Waiting. "You know, since we're stuck here," I said to him, "I think we should do more investigating. I'm determined to find some way to spoil Captain Drake's wicked plot, and if we really look, we're bound to find Lady Sarah *somewhere*."

I think Masou groaned softly but I wasn't sure. He wasn't very good at painting, so I found a bit of wood for mixing colours on, made some blue-green and set him doing the waves, which were easy.

I started to enjoy myself. It was hardly the same as embroidering a petticoat's false front, and the paints smelled terrible—I remember someone telling me once that white paint is made with mercury and sends alchemists mad—but it was interesting to try and make the scene look better. I decided I couldn't do much about the faces: they were just blobs of pink. But I was able to make the Queen's kirtle look something like it really does, and when I took a quick look about the cabin, I even found some pieces of paper left for kindling by the brazier—*and* a pen and ink on the desk.

At last I could scribble some notes on all that had happened to put in my daybooke later. I longed to write of my adventures, but of course I had not brought the daybooke with me because it is quite big and very precious and might be ruined by sea water—and what would Gregory the page want with a Maid of Honour's daybooke anyway? I would most likely have been taken for a spy—and thrown overboard or something terrible—had it been found!

Even writing a few notes took a while—and used up all the scraps of paper, which I folded and tucked in my pouch when I'd finished. Masou just shook his head at my lunacy and said nothing.

For a long time the painting and writing had kept my mind off a very serious problem, but I could not distract myself any longer. I realized I simply had to go to the jakes!

When I told Masou this he laughed and shook his head. Then he went outside to find the Boatswain. "Sir, may I show Gregory where the jakes are?" he asked.

The Boatswain, who was sitting outside like a guard, and drinking from a flask, nodded. "Mind you come back quick," he added.

Masou elbowed me. "I'll show you," he said.

We walked to the front end of the ship, where the painted beakhead jutted over the waves. Then we climbed onto it from the foredeck—which was hard, because it was going up and down quite a bit. One of the sailors was sitting there, his breeches untrussed and his bare bum over the side, as he peacefully smoked on a pipe.

I clutched Masou's hand. "Masou, there's somebody here," I gasped.

Masou squeezed my hand briefly and winked. "You can do it, Grace," he whispered, "I know you can." And then he swung himself down, unlacing as he did so, and sat next to the sailor with his bare bum hanging over the waves as well.

And I simply *had* to go. I was ready to burst. So I undid the lacing, then lowered myself down by one of the rope handles, until I was sitting on a plank with my bum bare like the other two and my shirt hanging down in front. My face was burning red, so hot I thought it would burst into flame, and even though I was so desperate, I couldn't do anything for ages. I just had to sit there with my privy parts getting colder and colder, hating Lady Sarah more and more each moment (although I knew it wasn't really her fault)!

Just as I was starting to relax, the sailor belched, farted, and sighed, banged the dottle out of his pipe into the sea, then heaved himself up and off the plank. "Best be quick, boys," he said. "No skiving on this ship, the Cap'n won't have it. He'll come down here looking for you himself, if needs must."

I could hear Masou snorting with suppressed laughter, though I don't know what he thought was so funny.

Once the sailor had gone, I concentrated hard on pretending to myself that I was just using a jakes on progress, and at last I managed to do what I had to do.

When I had got the laces done up again and heaved myself off the plank, I saw Masou waiting for me. "Never, never, never tell anyone . . . ," I whispered through gritted teeth.

"And have the Queen clap me in irons, throw me in the Tower, and then take my head off?" Masou replied, chuckling and shaking his head. "Never fear. But I wish you could see your face."

We went back to painting in the Great Cabin, with Masou still snorting with laughter every now and then. I don't know how sailors can bear it, I really don't.

A minute later the Boatswain came in and tapped me on the shoulder. "Come on," he said. "Time for vittles."

"I've got to clean the brushes first," I told him. Then I wiped them on the rag I'd been using to rub things out, and looked around for soapy water. The Boatswain pointed to another pot of bad-smelling stuff, so I dipped the brushes in that, and the paint did come off quite well. Once they were clean I left them to dry, and followed him and Masou back onto the deck.

"Well, he ain't lying about painting, at any rate," said the Boatswain to Mr. Newman. "He's done handsomely on the Captain's picture. Reckon they've both worked hard enough to get fed, now."

That was a relief. My stomach was so hollow it was making very strange *squeak-bubble* noises.

Mr. Newman nodded, so we went down steps and then more steps, down and down to the bilges where the Cook was. He was a scrawny man in a filthy shirt and jerkin and when I said "sir" to him, remembering what Masou had told me, he snorted. "You call me Cook, boy, that'll do. Squat over there to eat." He pointed to a space between two beer barrels. Then he slopped something that looked like vomit into two wooden bowls and gave them to Masou and me, along with a hunk of bread each and a big leather beaker of ale.

I drank my ale down at once, then looked at the stuff in the bowl. Masou was already hunkered down on his haunches, next to a barrel, throwing bread into his mouth. There wasn't room for us at any of the benches, and all the men were ignoring us.

"What is this?" I whispered, squatting next to him.

"Bacon and pease pottage," he whispered back. "As I am a Mussulman, I should not eat it, for the pig is unclean, but there is nothing else."

"Oh." I looked at it. I don't think I'd ever had it before. I tried a bit, and found it was very salty and strange tasting, but I was so hungry I ate half of it. Then somebody barged into me from behind and knocked me flying, so the food went on the deck.

"Watch where you're going!" I shouted, furious that my bit of bread was now on the dirty floor.

It was the sullen-looking boy again. "You watch

where you're sitting," he sneered. "You're in my way."

"No, I'm not," I defended myself. "You just did that on purpose—"

"You calling me a liar?" shouted the boy.

One of the men laughed, and tapped his neighbour. "Temper, Tom!" he called. But instead of doing something about the boy, they settled back to watch. Another man put down some pennies, and then another, and I suddenly realized they were laying bets on us.

Tom lifted up his fist and waved it under my nose. "I'm older'n you and I'm a sailor and you're not. So you do what I say."

Masou could see I was tempted to answer back and elbowed me hard. "Leave it," he whispered in my ear. "We don't want to get into a fight."

But then Tom kicked Masou's bowl over and shoved him flying into a barrel!

"What did you do that for?" I shouted at him.

"'Cause I choose," he spat. "'Cause I'm better'n you and that slave boy, and you better remember it."

I slapped him hard across the face. How *dare* he call Masou a slave?

He roared, and then hit me so hard on the side of the face, I fell to the ground. Tom had punched me! Me! A Maid of Honour to the Queen!

Masou cannoned into him, fists flying, and knocked him sideways. I stared for a second as I climbed to my feet, astonished at Masou, who was supposed to be the sensible one. Unfortunately, he isn't very big—or good at fighting—and that beefy Tom knocked him down with one of his big fists, and then kicked him.

That really made me lose my temper. Everything went all slow and cold. I'm not sure how I managed it, but I caught up some of the pottage from the floor and threw it in Tom's face, and then somehow I got my arm round his neck while he was trying to wipe it off, and started squeezing. He was terribly strong, and his arms flailed, but I just kept on squeezing while his face went red—and I hit his ear a couple of times too. . . .

Masou had climbed to his feet, with a wicked look on his face and his knife in his hand; at that, two of the men pounced on us, lifted Masou out of the way, and grabbed me by the shoulder.

"Let go," growled the one holding me. "Let go, right now."

After a moment, when the roaring in my ears had faded a bit, I did let go of Tom's neck. Tom fell to his knees, choking and gasping. Then he stood up, with a knife in his hand, too.

"Put it away, Tom," said the man behind me. "You got beat, now live with it."

Some of the other men clapped and started paying their bets. I thought we'd get some terrible punishment—but nobody said anything.

Masou picked his bread up off the floor before a hopeful rat got to it, and I did the same. Then I decided not to eat it because it had got trampled in the fight. The rat could have it, and welcome.

The three of us were ordered to clean up the mess made by the fight. I watched Tom like a hawk in case he tried to attack again, but he just scowled and did the minimum he could get away with. But I noticed that while he was cleaning, he carefully picked up all the spilled bits of bacon and put them on a bit of wood he had hidden in a corner. When he had gathered all he could find, he went to Cook and muttered something. I nearly sprained my ears trying to listen to them.

"Not again, Tom," Cook sighed.

"Captain said I could. It's for herself," Tom told him.

I was so excited I practically scrubbed a hole in the planks.

Cook shook his head and handed over a small

bowl of drinking water. "You're soft on her," he accused.

"I'm not soft!" grunted Tom, and he skulked off into the darkness.

I tried to catch Masou's eye, but he wasn't paying attention. I was desperate to talk to him. Both of them had said "her"! And this ship was full of men and boys only. Well, I was there, but nobody knew I was a girl. They must have been talking about Sarah!

I wished and wished I could follow Tom to wherever he was taking the supplies, but I couldn't. Cook was watching us. I made careful note of which direction he had gone in, and that was all I could do—which was terribly frustrating. Of course, it was awful for Sarah, being fed leftover bacon that had been on the floor, and nothing but water to drink. I could only think that Drake was sorely vexed with her—Sarah is very trying, and perhaps she had refused to give in to his wicked plans! But Masou and I weren't doing too well, either. My face was puffing up in a bruise, and Masou had a split lip.

As we finished working, Cook kept shaking his head and chuckling to himself. "Don't think any of 'em expected to see you give Tom a run for his money like that," he said to me, shaking his head. "You've got some spirit in you, lad. No wonder you've run away to sea. I done the same myself, in my time."

I saw a great opportunity: Cook would likely know everything that went on aboard the *Judith*. So I pretended to be interested in hearing how he had run away to sea—and had to listen to a very long and unlikely tale about how he'd "nearly got sunk and drownded with the King's Great Ship and then fought the French hand to hand." I made impressed noises as he told me, then, when he'd finished, I risked a question. "Do you know what the Captain's up to on this voyage, Cook?" I asked casually.

"Oh, aye, hoping for some plunder, eh?" Cook assumed. He tapped his nose. "Well, Captain did put to sea in an almighty hurry—we'd not even fully finished loading our supplies. He might've caught wind of whatever it was Captain Derby was hurrying to find. But nobody knows for sure. Captain's not said yet what we're up to."

I decided to risk another. "Um . . . have you ever known anyone . . . bring a woman to sea on the *Judith,* Cook?" I asked, busily scrubbing the pot in my hands.

Cook chuckled. "Oh, aye," he said—it seemed to be his favourite phrase. My heart leaped, thinking he was going to tell me of Lady Sarah! "There was that Sam Pike," he went on. My heart sank again. "See, he was lately wed, and desperate for to keep his wife close by him. So he smuggled her aboard dressed as a sailor and she hid in the cable tiers, and the sail locker, and even the brig. And when the Captain came round for his inspections, you never saw such a flurry, what with Sam and his mates shifting her out of the hold and into the galley one step ahead of him. I did laugh. Course, she got tired of it and fell asleep one night in Sam's bed, and the Captain found her . . . Oh, aye, he was fit to be tied, was the Captain . . . Would have flogged Sam, he said, only he was such a good topman. Mrs. Pike spent the rest of the voyage shut up in a cabin, sewing, and couldn't wait to get off the ship when we came home to Plymouth."

Cook shook his head again, grinning. "Oh, aye, the men are always trying it on, but the Captain, he just won't have it. He said, clear as clear, he said, 'I'd as soon have a raging bull on my poop deck as a woman stowed away in the cable tiers for the men to fight and grieve over.' That's what he said."

I grinned back, all the while thinking what a hypocrite Drake was—abducting Lady Sarah without a by-your-leave, and then keeping her hidden away somewhere aboard ship! I tried one last line of investigation: "Oh," I said, "it's just that I thought I saw a woman in one of the cabins, Cook. Very pretty, red hair, with a figure . . ." I made a curvy shape in the air, as I'd seen gentlemen do about Sarah when they didn't know I was watching.

Cook laughed and swatted me lightly with a ladle. "You're too young to be thinking sinful thoughts, Greg. You get your back into cleaning these here pots—that'll settle you down for the night."

Masou shook his head as we worked away at cleaning the black iron pots with sand. It was really hard work, and quite stinky, and my hands got sore from the sand. I kept thinking of Lady Sarah, in irons in the brig—which was where I thought she must be hidden since few seemed aware of her presence and she was being fed on scraps. But by the time we finished, all I could think of was how lucky she was to be sitting down and not having to work. At last Cook said we could stop.

I was exhausted. "Do you know where we are to sleep, Cook?" I asked him.

"Here, it's the last space we've got," he said, pointing at the gap between the barrels where Masou and I had eaten. "I've counted every onion and cabbage, and if there's even one missing in the morning, I'll beat you."

"But what if the rats eat them, Cook?" I asked.

"That's why you're here," he replied. "Keep 'em away, and you won't get beaten, see?" He seemed quite friendly now—he even gave us a filthy blanket to share. Then he hung a candle-lantern from a beam so we could see the rats, and left us.

I lay down awkwardly, top to tail with Masou. I'd slept on a straw pallet on the floor when on progress, but never on the *actual* floor! The planks were really hard, and I was so tired my head was spinning, plus my ear was hurting and my cheek felt like a sore pillow—and bits of me were all bruised where Tom's fists had flailed. This adventure was turning out to be a very uncomfortable one—even for a Lady Pursuivant.

Masou's lip was swollen, too, but he seemed to find something funny, chuckling away to himself.

"What?" I asked crossly.

He shook his head. "Where did Lady Grace Cavendish learn to fight like that?" he mused.

I scowled, because I was a bit embarrassed about it.

Masou reached over and patted my leg. "You make quite a boy, Gregory," he said. Then he put his head on his arm and seemed to fall asleep at once.

I kept hearing skittering in the shadows, and then a pair of small eyes shone red in the lamplight. I threw a bit of squashed bread at them.

Masou snored gently and annoyingly beside me, but I think that even if the planks had been soft as pillows, I would not have been able to sleep—because I kept thinking of Tom taking food to someone who was a "her"! Who could it be except Sarah? Cook must have been lying to me. I had to find her. And I could not leave further search a moment longer!

I considered waking Masou to let him know what I was up to, but he was in such a deep sleep, I decided against it. And anyway, it would be easier to creep around, and hide, on my own.

I got up very quietly, left my boots and socks off, and crept along to the ladder.

The hatch was down, but not bolted. I pushed it up slowly, hoisted myself out, and crept along again.

I knew, from listening to the sailors talking, that there'd be a watch kept on deck, but below decks was different. Down here, the sailors who weren't on watch were bundled up, snoring, all over the place—and every deck smelled worse than the last—of sweat mainly, but also of onions and beer and salt fish, and that thing which happens to your bowels when you eat too much pease pudding.

I went all the way aft to the stern. We hadn't been able to search the rear of the ship properly before we were shut in the sail locker. I was praying that more of the doors might be open—and some of them were—but they were storerooms with nobody in them.

There was a hatch next to the capstan and I opened it and peered in. I could see thick anchor ropes in the shadows. They smelled horrible: salty mud and rotten seaweed. "Lady Sarah?" I called softly. "Are you there?"

But there was no reply, just the creaking of the ship and the clopping of the water, and loud snoring coming from somewhere else.

Further along, I found a door with a big lock on it and guessed it was the brig, because it had a tiny hatch to pass food through. Heart thudding, I opened the hatch—and the smell from within almost knocked me down by itself! Hell's teeth! Now I hoped Lady Sarah was *not* in there! Bracing myself, I put my face to the hatch again, and called softly.

There was no answer, and I was relieved that Lady Sarah was not languishing in such a hell-hole—but where else was there to look? I wondered desperately.

Then I remembered Cook's story of Sam Pike—and how he had moved his wife around the ship, while hiding her. Captain Drake didn't have to keep Sarah in one place either, did he? I rolled my eyes. There was no help for it—I couldn't possibly go to sleep thinking about that. I would have to search everywhere afresh.

So I crept forward again, looking carefully in all the cabins, hiding in the shadows when some sailors came by.

I found myself outside the sail locker again. I opened the door and, just for a second, I thought I'd found her. There was a candle guttering on the floor and someone lying curled up there. "Lady Sarah?" I whispered cautiously.

The shape on the floor moved. By then I had realized it was too big and the wrong shape to be Lady

Sarah. It was that ugly bully, Tom. Why he was sleeping there, I didn't know, but I didn't want to get into another fight with him, so I turned to creep away.

Suddenly a hand caught my shoulder and slammed me against the wall. "What you doing here?" Tom growled.

I thought quickly, and said the first thing that came into my head: "I . . . I've come to see the kittens." Then I shut my mouth in horror. What would he think? He'd guess I was a girl now, surely!

Tom loomed over me. I couldn't see his face in the candle shadows. "If you're coming to drown them kittens—" he began.

"Of course not!" I cried, shocked at such a thought. "I just came to see them."

The big hand let go of my shoulder. "That right, then?"

"Yes. What are *you* doing here?" I demanded, remembering how Masou always fared better by standing up for himself.

Tom drew himself up straighter. "I'm guarding, that's what."

"What?" I asked, sounding very stupid.

"I'm not letting any of them sailors drown 'er kittens." He was scowling now.

"Well, of course you shouldn't," I said. "Who would want to do a thing like that?"

"Some of 'em," Tom muttered. "They reckon it's a bit of fun. But I'm not having it. And I don't *care* if they say Tom Webster's soft. Them kittens is stayin' safe until they can go to other ships. We've got plenty of rats for 'em."

I was outraged that some might see it as sport to harm the kittens. "You're *not* soft, Tom," I said, forgetting I'd fought him. "You're doing what's right."

He grunted and stood there, looking at me for a while. "You want to see 'em?"

I squatted down and peered next to the candle in its holder. There were the kittens, lying in a heap on their mother, who was purring softly.

"Don't try and stroke her, she'll scratch you," Tom warned, smiling fondly. "She's a fierce one."

I looked for a while longer. Then I had to ask him. "Tom, why did you fight me and my friend?"

Tom shrugged. "Bull's-eye Jarvis bet me a shilling I couldn't beat the two of you, so I took him on."

"But why?" I persisted. "We never did either of you any harm."

"I can't let them think I'm soft, can I?" Tom replied gruffly.

I shook my head. It all sounded daft to me: Tom didn't have to fight complete strangers to show he was tough. I thought much better of him now, though—and so would Masou. "Well, a Knight of the Queen also protects the weak, and is regarded as the bravest of the brave," I said.

"What do you know about it?" sniffed Tom.

"I was apprenticed in the Queen's Wardrobe, it's a Department of State," I told him.

"Is that why you talk funny?" Tom asked.

"Er . . . yes," I replied. "Anyway, as I was saying, a Knight of the Queen should be brave in battle against the strong to defend the weak, and gentle with the weak themselves. That's how you know he's a gentleman."

"Oh," Tom mumbled. It looked as if he needed to think hard about that one.

While he was doing so, I decided I might as well sidle away. He didn't stop me: he was too busy frowning with the effort of thinking.

I did look in a few more places, but had no luck, and by now I was feeling sadly discouraged. I was so sure Tom had been taking the bacon scraps to

Lady Sarah, but obviously they had been for the ship's cat instead—and I was no nearer to finding Sarah. My eyes felt hot and sore, and they started dropping shut by themselves. Wearily I climbed back down to the galley and lay down next to Masou under the blanket, even though I knew I would never ever get to sleep on such a hard floor, with all the smells and snores and strange sounds of the ship.

Almost instantly, it seemed, it was morning! A bell was clanging, and I felt just awful. I hurt all over. I seemed to have lumps and bumps on every bit of me, and my hands and shoulders ached.

Masou woke then—and he seemed to be in better shape. I suppose he is more used to climbing and brawling than I!

Cook came to make breakfast—which was the most horrible grey salty porridge, with more ale and bread. This time I ate the bread, which was like leather, and gave Masou my porridge. Then there was a clanging and a banging, and all the sailors rushed up the ladder.

Cook pointed at it. "All hands on deck," he said. "Captain wants to talk to the men. You want to know what we're doing—now's your chance to find out. Up you go."

Masou and I went up to the main deck and stood at the back, behind the tallest sailors we could find, in case the Captain saw me and recognized me. From here, we couldn't see Drake at all, but Masou was happy just to listen to his speech. I wanted to see Drake so I peered round the sailors and managed to get a glimpse of him.

There he was, standing on the very top, aftmost deck, his handsome face both happy and serious. He should be happy! Probably he was going to marry Lady Sarah now. I scowled at him heavily, even though he couldn't see me. How dare he do it? What an evil man—and I'd thought he was kind.

"Well, men," he said, and his Devonshire voice carried the length of the ship without his seeming to shout. "I don't doubt you're wondering why we put to sea in such an almighty hurry!"

There was a rumble of answering "Aye, sir"s.

"I'm not sure what's afoot," Captain Drake went on, "but I know that Captain Derby put to sea a day early, and I'd like to have a sniff of whatever he's after. Could be a nice fat Spanish Netherland merchant, could be sea beggars, could even be a Spanish treasure ship gone astray."

Most of the men cheered.

"So we're making the same heading as he. I know the places where he likes to cruise and if we keep a sharp lookout, we might see his prize afore he does." Drake smiled—well, he showed his teeth, really—and smacked his fist in his palm. "Then we'll snap her up!"

All the men cheered and waved their fists at that.

"I've a letter of marque from the Queen—that's Her Majesty Queen Elizabeth, her very self!" he shouted, waving a piece of paper. At the Queen's name everyone cheered again. "So we can take any ship we don't like the look of, so long as she ain't English nor Hollander nor Allemayne."

Really loud cheering.

"Now, I'm telling you what I heard," Drake added. "I heard there's a Spanish man-of-war out in the Narrow Seas, carrying the foul Duke of Alva's letter of marque, and he's been a-taking of our ships, what's more. Now we can't be having that, can we, boys?"

Roars of "No, sir, we'll have they Spaniels to our breakfast!"

"So keep a sharp lookout and be ready, and there's prize money fat and bright just waiting for the taking!" Drake finished.

Wildly enthusiastic cheering.

Masou and I looked at each other. What did Drake think he was doing, going on a privateering expedition with Lady Sarah on board? When was he going to marry her?

"What happened to that pretty Court fish you pulled out of the water the other day, Captain?" asked the Carpenter with a knowing grin, as if he'd read my mind.

Captain Drake paused and frowned. "I'll have none of the likes of you making no comments about any fair lady of Her Majesty's Court, Jim Woolley, you hear?"

"Aye, sir," said the man, sounding abashed. "Sorry, sir."

"I'll tell you the truth, men!" shouted Drake. "I'll not deny I laid suit to her for she'm the fairest I've ever seen, with all her red hair and her pretty ways. But just afore we sailed, she wrote me and told me, I'm not rich enough for her—and that's fair enough, for she's gently bred and expensive for to keep, what's more. So we're out to get rich this voyage, lads, fast as we can, and then I can go courting again with a hatful of gold!"

They all hooted and cheered at that, while Masou and I gaped at each other.

Captain Drake turned away and went to talk to Mr. Newman.

Masou and I got shouted at to go below and help Cook. While I cleared away the officers' mess, scrubbing the tables with silver sand and lye, I tried to think. It didn't make any sense. What was Drake talking about, going courting with a hatful of gold? He didn't need to if he already had Lady Sarah on board. . . .

Then Tom came and grunted at us. "Mr. Newman wants you," he said. "Best go quick."

Up on the deck, Masou and I knuckled our foreheads to Mr. Newman.

"Captain wants a sharp lookout kept," he told us. "You go up to the foremast top and stay there, until I tell you to come down or you see anything at all—a sail, a sea monster, anything."

As we went over to the rail, I turned to Masou. "I don't believe it, he—"

Somebody shoved us.

"What are you doing yapping away?" snarled the wide man who had first discovered us on the ship. "You get aloft and keep watch, and you'd better do it right."

"Aye, sir," I said, swallowing hard. I was almost

pleased we were to go up the mast again, so I could talk to Masou in peace! But Hell's teeth! Those awful ratlines again . . .

There was no help for it, so we climbed up and up and up—and I struggled up and backwards and over the side of the top again, grabbing for ropes to hold onto.

When I'd got my breath back I could see that Tom was over on the mainmast fighting top, shading his eyes to keep a lookout. We squinted into the distance, too, me facing one way, Masou the other. At last we could talk.

I spoke first. "I think that perhaps Captain Drake does not have Lady Sarah at all!" I said.

Masou looked as if he'd been thinking just the same thing. "Well, we've seen no sign of her any-where on the ship, have we?" he muttered. "And after what Drake said in his speech . . ."

I nodded miserably. It made my stomach swoop to think we'd got ourselves trapped on a privateering ship for nothing! "So where can she be?" I asked, full of frustration.

Masou shrugged and spread his hands wide.

I took out the forged letter, which I still had in my doublet, and squinted at it. Somehow, I had read the evidence wrongly. But if Captain Drake hadn't taken Lady Sarah, who had? I sighed heavily. "I must tell Captain Drake what has been going on," I admitted. "Maybe he can take us back to Tilbury and there will be news there of Lady Sarah." I stuffed the letter away again, went to the side, and started sliding backwards over it, feeling for the ropes with my toes.

"What if he throws you in the brig?" Masou demanded anxiously.

"It can't be helped. I've still got to try," I puffed, letting myself down carefully. "You keep watch, so we don't get into more trouble."

I climbed the rest of the way, sliding a bit because I was in such a hurry. Mr. Newman was busy with a big sail at the front of the ship, so I dodged two sailors and ran to the back deck (sorry, aft), where I wasn't supposed to go at all. Facing the door of the Great Cabin, feeling sick with fright, I knocked.

"Enter," came the Captain's voice.

I opened the door and peered inside apprehensively. "Captain, sir, please may I talk with you?"

Drake was bending over charts on the table, but in fact he wasn't looking at them, he was staring at a letter. He glanced up and frowned at me.

I grabbed my hat off my head, came into the cabin, shut the door, and bowed low. "Sir, I really must talk with you," I said.

"Who are you, boy?"

He hadn't recognized me! I hesitated. Should I tell him who I really was? No, not yet. He would be surprised half to death—and he had to concentrate on what I had to say. "I'm Gregory, sir."

"Ah yes, the stowaway who's a painter," Drake remembered. "You did well on the paintings, lad. I'll have you do some more for me once we're out of dangerous waters."

"Thank you, sir." I thought fast. "But, begging your pardon, I'm really a page. Lady Sarah Bartelmy's page, sir . . ."

At the mention of Lady Sarah's name, Drake's blue eyes bored into me like needles.

"She's missing, sir," I continued. "And I thought at first that she might be on this ship, so I came to find her. . . ."

Drake frowned, and those fiery blue eyes chilled to ice. I felt terrified. Being frowned at by Drake was like being hit in the forehead.

"And then the ship set sail, and . . . um . . . here I am . . . ," I finished. "Only Lady Sarah sent this letter to the Queen, sir. . . ." I hurried forward, deciding it wouldn't hurt to be a bit courtly, as if I really were a page, and went down on one knee to give him the letter, as if he were an earl or a duke.

He snatched the letter from me in irritation, but as he read it, his ruddy face paled.

"It's a forgery, sir, I know that much," I told him. "My Lady Sarah pens her *y*s quite different."

Drake's face was a mixture of puzzlement and fury. I thought he might start shouting at me, but instead he handed me the letter he had been reading when I came in.

I read it quickly. This is what it said:

Palace of Placentia, Greenwich
The seventh day of May, in the Year of Our Lord 1569

Sir,

My noble father hath written unto me this day that he hath found for me a husband of a like blood and land as myself. Our dalliance must be at an end for my revered parents would never countenance that I should so disparage myself as to wed a man of lesser breeding and wealth.

Sarah, Lady Bartelmy

I squinted at the *y*s—and sure enough, they had no curly tails. "This is a forgery, too," I declared.

"But the pearl bracelet I gave her was returned with the letter," Drake said slowly. "And now she's missing, you say?"

"Yes, sir," I confirmed. "My friend Masou saw her being helped on board a boat at the Greenwich river steps."

"Where is this Masou?" Drake demanded.

"He's up the mast, keeping watch, sir," I replied. "We came on board the night before last, sir, trying to find Lady Sarah—only we got locked in the sail locker by accident, and Mr. Newman thinks we're stowaways so he sent us up the mast—"

"Stay there!" Drake commanded, already striding out of his cabin.

Just at that moment I heard a faint shout.

"Sail!" It was Masou's voice. "Sail, ho!" he shouted again.

I rushed out on deck, too.

"Where away?" shouted the Boatswain.

"That way!" came Masou's faint reply. He was much higher than the top—he was right up where we'd freed the banner, clinging like a monkey and pointing.

"Mr. Newman, make more sail!" Captain Drake bellowed.

I was puzzled—surely they didn't have time to make sails, and anyway, there were plenty in the sail locker. But then I saw that Drake meant the crew to open up more sails on the masts, to catch more wind and move the ship faster.

He jumped up to the rail and started to climb the ratlines, smoothly and surely as if he were just climbing some stairs. I scrambled up after him, after tucking both letters in my doublet.

Puffing and clawing over the side of the fighting top, I saw Drake's boots, and then felt him lift me up by my jerkin. He didn't seem to mind that I hadn't stayed where I was told. He was staring into the distance, where there were two white notches on the horizon. Masou was sliding down from his high perch, looking scared and worried.

"Tell me exactly what you saw when you watched Lady Sarah get in the boat at Greenwich," Drake ordered Masou. "Whom was she with?"

"You're Captain Drake, sir?" Masou asked, sounding very surprised.

"Aye, son, that's my name."

"Well, she was with a taller man than you, sir, with light hair," Masou told him.

I stared at Masou, incredulous. He hadn't recognized the man helping Lady Sarah into the boat as being someone other than Captain Drake? Then I realized that Masou had never seen Drake before now. It had been *I* who had told *him* that the man in the boat was Captain Drake. Because Mary and I had assumed it to be. . . .

"Straw-coloured hair? Green woollen suit?" demanded Drake, his face intent.

"Yes, sir." Masou nodded. "No chin."

"Hugh Derby," Drake concluded grimly.

Horrified, I realized what had really happened: *Derby* had abducted Lady Sarah, and had tried to make it look like Captain Drake had!

The Captain leaned casually over the edge of the platform to bellow some orders at Mr. Newman, who was staring up at us. I wasn't sure what the orders were about, because they were entirely in Sailorish—something about putting bonnets on the sails and then something about a direction. . . .

"And Mr. Newman . . . ," Drake added.

"Aye, sir?" Mr. Newman asked.

"Clear for battle stations," Drake finished coolly.

Mr. Newman's face lit up. "Aye aye, sir!"

The ship below us erupted like a stepped-on ants' nest—people were running everywhere—but it was a very organized sort of chaos. Soon more sails were unwrinkling themselves, and the yards—they're the wooden beams that support the sails—were being pulled into different positions by ropes—called lines.

The *Judith* began moving faster through the water, and changed direction towards the two distant ships that Masou had spotted.

"So Captain Derby took her," murmured Drake thoughtfully. "And tried to lay the blame on me."

Both Masou and I nodded.

Drake looked up. "I want the topsail set," he said. "We're here so we'll do it. Up you go."

My heart lurched. "I don't know what to do, sir," I told him. "I'm a page, not a sailor."

"I know that. I'll tell you what to do," Drake assured me.

He followed us up the ratlines to where the top-yard crossed the mast. Then he told us to get our toes on the toe-rope and lean over the yard and shuffle along. Masou did it first. It's a tree, I told myself; it's a tree branch and there are cherries in an awkward place. I love cherries. So I gulped again, leaned over the yard, felt for the rope, and sort of slid along on my stomach. Everything whirled for a moment.

"Don't forget to breathe, lad," I heard Drake's voice say—and it sounded as though he were sauntering in a garden. He was next to the mast, busy with ropes. "Now you'll see a reef knot in front of you. Untie it, loosen the rope, and let the sail drop."

Yes, there was a knotted rope in front of me, holding the sail tight to the yard, which was rocking wildly. It's a tree, I said to myself again, just a tree. I fumbled at the knot, picking at it one-handed, the other hand holding tight to the wooden yard. At last, after I broke a nail, it came undone.

"Come back now," said Drake.

I slid back along the yard, grabbed the ratlines, and stepped back onto them, wobbling from sheer fright. Drake caught my shoulder and held me steady until I could catch my breath and get a proper grip. Then he did more mysterious stuff with rope, shouted, and the topsail plopped out and was pulled taut from below. The ship leaned over further and picked up speed.

Drake started climbing down again. Masou and I followed, although I was still shaking.

Back on the fighting top once more, it felt almost as good as a deck.

"So you're Lady Sarah's page and you came to help her, though you know nothing of the sea?" Drake asked, staring at me shrewdly. I nodded.

Masou was listening to this with fascination.

Drake turned to him next. "And you came to help your friend here?" he asked. Masou nodded, too.

Then Drake held out his hand for us to shake, so we did, fumbling with surprise. "I like courage and enterprise in any man, and faithfulness in any friend," he said soberly. I felt my heart swell with pride. "Can either of you use weapons?" he then asked.

"I can shoot with a bow, sir," I said, which is true, since I've been taught archery to go hunting with the Queen—except I've never had the heart to shoot anything alive. But I'm quite good at targets.

"A knife," said Masou, eyes narrowing. "I can throw a knife."

"Hm," said Drake with a smile, "so can I. We'll have a contest one day." He shaded his eyes and peered out over the water. Suddenly he grinned most ferociously. "Unless I've gone blind, I'd say that smaller ship is Captain Derby's *Silver Arrow,*" he observed. "And he's in trouble by the looks of it, for that larger one is the Spaniard that's been taking of our ships."

"But aren't they both flying the English flag?" I asked, squinting in the same direction.

"Aye, well, just a little entertainment for us,"

Drake said. "Me, I'd say that bigger ship's rigging is from Vigo—Spain."

He leaned over and shouted to Mr. Newman again. A flag travelled up the mainmast and flapped in the wind—I recognized the double eagle of the Habsburgs of Spain.

"Something to entertain them, too," said Drake with a laugh. "Now, boys, my thinking is that they Spaniels are shaping to take Captain Derby's ship, which would be a pity seeing it's his only livelihood."

"And what about Lady Sarah?" I asked anxiously.

"Derby was smitten with her, I know that, for he nearly challenged me to a duel for sending her that bracelet," Drake explained. "And so I think he did, in sooth, take her by force." His eyes then turned all soft. "I hope such a delicate lady stays out of harm's way in the next hour," he added.

He wasn't looking at me, thank goodness, he was staring into space, mooning about Sarah Copperlocks Bartelmy again. Hell's teeth! Even as his ship was preparing to go into battle! What *is* it men see in her?

I was more worried about being caught up in a battle—for myself *and* Lady Sarah! I could see the two ships in the distance drawing steadily closer. A mixture of fear and excitement made my stomach feel like a posset-cup. My mouth was all dry, too. Was there really going to be a sea battle? I couldn't believe it. How had it happened?

"Now," said Captain Drake, holding onto a line. "Two likely boys like you, I expect you'll want to be right in the thick of the fighting. Alas, I must disappoint you, and there'll be no gainsaying me. I can't have you down on the deck, for you might get in the way of us boarding. But you can fight from up here, understand?"

Masou and I both nodded—me because my mouth was so dry, my lips were stuck together. Want to be in the thick of the fight? In on a battle? Me? What if I got hurt or killed? (I thought killed might be better—much less embarrassing.)

"Masou, you run down and fetch a bow and quivers for your mate, and some fire pots and slow match for yourself, then come straight back up again," Drake ordered.

"Aye, sir," croaked Masou, then he swung himself over the side to go down.

"You, lad," said Drake, staring at me very hard. "What's your name?"

"Gra—Gregory," I stammered. I'd nearly told him my name was Grace!

"Hm. Well, Gregory, there's more to you than meets the eye, something not quite right. I know I've seen you before, but I cannot place you."

"Maybe you saw me attending my Lady Sarah," I said, trying not to squeak with nerves.

"Perhaps," the Captain acknowledged. "At any rate, I can't put my finger on it. Are you dealing straight with me, lad?"

"I came to find Lady Sarah," I said. "I never meant to stow—"

"No, I believe you on that matter," Drake cut in. "It's something else."

I felt as if his eyes were drilling holes in me.

He stared for a little longer and then seemed to come to a decision. "Aye, well, I've not leisure for it now, but you'll tell me after, if you're spared." He wasn't asking a question, he was stating a fact.

I swallowed hard.

There was a sound of climbing, and Masou reappeared, with bags and a bow slung over his back, and some slow match wrapped around his wrist.

"Ah, Masou, well done. Listen to what I want you to do." The Captain had his tinder box out of his belt pouch and was lighting a candle, and then, carefully, the slow match. "Here's your slow match— keep it away from the fire pots. Light the fuses one at a time, then throw the fire pot nice and easy into the rigging of the Spaniel ship, understand?"

"Aye, sir," Masou said.

The Captain then turned to me. "Now, Gregory, these are fire arrows. Light them from Masou's slow match and aim 'em for the sails, understand? When we're grappled for boarding, shoot the ordinary arrows at the Spaniels, but once I lead the men across the boarding plank, stop shooting, for you might shoot me!"

"Aye, sir," I said.

Drake smiled, his eyes serious and yet somehow also full of excitement. He seemed to be looking forward to the fight.

He clapped both of us on the back, then swung himself over the edge of the top and slid, hand over hand, down a rope.

Masou and I stared at each other, and then Masou crowed with laughter and punched the air with his fist. "I always wanted to be in a battle!" he shouted. "I am a warrior—and the finest acrobat in Mr. Somers's troop. *Allah akhbar!*"

I think boys—men—are all complete Bedlamites. They're all mad. Adventures are one thing, but a battle! My heart was thudding away, my palms all sweaty. I needed to make water, but I couldn't on the draughty top.

To have something to do, I got the bow Masou had brought up to me and strung it. It was quite small and not too stiff—I had bent stronger bows before. But I was scared of shooting a fire arrow. There were twelve of them, with pitch-soaked wadding wrapped round the head and a lump of clay behind the fletching to balance them. There were twenty-four of the ordinary arrows, too—along with a bracer and gloves, which I put on.

Then I noticed her, the mother cat, climbing determinedly up the rigging towards me, with a kitten in her mouth. I stared disbelievingly. What was she doing?

I realized she must have been ousted from her nice warm nest in the sail locker, and now she was looking for a safe place. I heard a squeak nearby and looked round—there were three little furry, big-eyed faces peering over the side of a coil of rope just next to the mast. I stared at the mother as she climbed higher and higher, clinging with her claws. As if I didn't have enough to worry about already! Once she almost slipped, but a sailor who was lacing another bit to the bottom of a sail to make it bigger just caught her in his hand and placed her higher up. And on she climbed with her kitten.

A drum started beating down on the deck. *Boom-boom-boom, boom-da-da boom-da-da boom!* There was something wild and dangerous and threatening about the beat—it made my heart beat along with it. The sailors were singing something, growling deep and loud. It sounded very fierce.

The two other ships were quite close now, and they were joined together by a plank and grappling hooks. You could easily see that one of the ships was much bigger—it was flying a Habsburg double eagle now and it had three masts. The smaller ship only had two masts—and a big pile of wreckage lay on the deck where half of one had fallen down. There were white splintery scrapes where cannon-balls had hit, and what looked like bloodstains on the deck. Some kind of swirling battle was raging on the smaller ship, the *Silver Arrow*, but a few of the fighters were scrambling back across ropes to the Spanish ship.

I looked up at the *Judith*'s mainmast. The Habsburg double eagle was coming down and the red-on-white Cross of St. George was just flying free.

The mother cat appeared over the edge of the fighting top and leaped into the coil of rope, where she settled down. All the kittens started feeding and kneading her with their paws.

BOOM!

It was the loudest noise I'd ever heard, and I nearly fell off the fighting top with fright. One of the guns on the deck had fired. Drake was on the poop deck, bellowing more Sailorish orders. The yards moved, and sent our ship leaning in towards the other two. Another gun fired. The *Judith* sailed past the grappled ships, on the other side of the Spaniard. Oh, good, I thought, maybe no battle. But then the guns poking out of the side of the *Judith* started firing.

BOOM! BOOM! BOOM! BOOM! BOOM!

The whole ship quivered. Clouds of smoke made it look as if we were sitting on a little island above the clouds. There was screaming from the Spanish ship. One of its cannons fired back, and splinters showered from the place where the cannonball had struck the *Judith*.

Drake yelled up to us. Masou licked his lips, lit a fire pot from the slow match, and lobbed it carefully into the Spanish ship's fighting top. Flames rose up, followed by hissing as someone doused it with water. I nocked an arrow and Masou blew on the glowing slow match and lit the pitch-soaked wadding. It felt very hot, even through the leather glove. I felt the heat on my face, and fired without really aiming, high in an arch, just to get rid of it. I don't think I hit anything.

Masou was already throwing again. I glimpsed Tom firing arrows, too, so I lit another one of mine, aimed for a sail as a target—and hit it. I watched the fire catch and spread.

Every so often, Tom would stare wildly in our direction. I wondered why, until suddenly I smelled burning close by. I stared wildly around. The cat was cowering deep in the coil of rope, with her kittens beneath her—too late she must have realized what an unwise place she had chosen. When one kitten tried to struggle out to look, she whacked it with a paw and pushed it back. Her fur was all on end and she was hissing. She was so small and so brave, it made me feel better at once.

I smelled a horrible stink. Some of the tarry ropes in our rigging were burning—there was a fire arrow stuck there from the boys in the Spanish ship's top. They jeered in Spanish—they hadn't noticed that their own sail was burning.

"Masou!" I gasped, pointing at the flames in the rigging.

"Later," said Masou, narrowing his eyes and lobbing another fire pot into the crow's nest of the other ship.

I couldn't believe he was ignoring the fact that we might get burned to death! But I lit another fire arrow, too—fired, and fired again, always aiming away from the people. I just didn't want to kill anyone, not even a Spaniard. They hadn't done me any harm, even if they were trying to now!

Masou had thrown all the fire pots and had started several fires in the Spanish ship's rigging. Now he took one of the bags of sand hanging above the fighting top platform, and climbed out along the ropes to get at the fire in our own rigging, which was now spreading.

I watched in horror as he hung by his knees, slit the sandbag, and poured sand into the place where the flames were leaping, then banged the place with the empty bag, until the flames were all gone and only smoke was left. Arrows fired by the Spanish whizzed past him, and something banged and cracked splinters off the wood right next to me. It was a musket ball. Suddenly I realized properly that the Spaniards really were trying to kill us!

I grabbed my bow and fired back at them, so they had to stop shooting and duck down. I was furious. How dare they try to shoot Masou like that! As soon as I paused, more Spanish arrows came flying over, and I had to duck myself. Fortunately, the Spanish didn't aim very well, and several of their arrows stuck in the wood—which was good, because I could pull them out and shoot them back.

Next there was a dreadful grinding crash, and the whole ship shook like a leaf. Masou cried out. I peered over again. The rope he'd been hanging from had suddenly given way—he'd caught another one and was hanging by his hands, dangling over the deck, fifty feet below!

I heard a slam—they'd dropped the boarding plank onto the Spaniard's rail.

"Follow me!" roared Drake, and he ran across the plank with his sword in his right hand and his pistol in his left, followed by his drummer hammering the drum, and a horde of sailors, all waving short swords and axes. Some of them were swinging across from the rigging onto the boarding nets, and climbing up— while the Spanish sailors tried to stab them with spears. The two ships rocked and jolted and there was the most terrible clanging and screaming.

Nobody was going to help Masou except me. So I squinted at the rope he was dangling from, trying to work out which one it was, out of all the many ropes criss-crossing the sails. Masou wasn't far from the top of the big sail below us. At last I identified it— and luckily, the other end was attached to the fighting top. I unwound it part way, passed it round the mast, and then, holding my breath, unwound the rest of it and let it out a little at a time. Masou was very heavy, despite being small. I couldn't possibly pull him up, so I eased him down bit by bit, while trying to keep away from the flying arrows. "I'm letting you down to the yard!" I shouted.

Masou was staying absolutely still to make it easier for me, reaching with his toes for the yard. Once he touched it, I felt the weight lighten. I lowered him a little more, and then—I couldn't believe my eyes!—he just let go of the rope he'd been clinging to, and ran along the yard to the ratlines! He ran. Along a pole fifty feet up! And then, when he got to the ratlines, he reached out and swung onto them, then climbed up them to the fighting top. "Phew!" he said, and mopped his brow theatrically.

That was when I burst into tears, because I'd been so scared for him. He gave me a hug.

When I'd recovered, we peered over the top again—I'd run out of arrows by then. I saw Tom staring anxiously over again, so I waved and shouted, "The cat's all right! She's here!" I pointed to where the mother cat was still protecting her kittens in her coil of rope—thank goodness no arrows or fire pots had fallen there. After a moment, Tom smiled.

"What was that about?" asked Masou, frowning in puzzlement. "Why are you waving at that fat pig?"

"Oh, he's not so bad," I said. "Somebody put him up to bullying us. He's been looking after the kittens."

Masou blinked and then shook his head, looking bewildered.

When we looked over at the battle again, the huge swirling mass of fighting men had changed. It had now split into three groups, because the men on the *Silver Arrow* were helping Drake's men, and the Spanish were getting pushed back to the front part of their own ship. I saw something white flapping on the Spanish ship, and pointed it out to Masou.

The next moment, all the clanging and fighting and noise began to fade, then stopped. All I could hear was a lot of men panting and gasping for breath, and someone moaning in pain.

"Come on!" said Masou. "The Spanish have surrendered."

We climbed down in a hurry, and found that the men on the *Arrow* were cutting the Spaniard grappling ropes and trying to heave up the spiked boarding plank. I could see a tall man on the poop deck, shouting orders as Drake did, though he was too far away for me to be sure it was Derby.

Suddenly Drake was shouting orders, too. He stood on the rail of the highest deck on the Spaniard ship and jumped straight across onto the *Arrow*. Some of his men followed him. Meanwhile, Mr. Newman was aiming a pistol at the Spanish Captain, who was laying down his weapons.

Desperate to know what was happening, Masou and I picked our way across the deck, passing a man lying dead, an axe in his head. It made me want to be sick, so I tried not to look.

Masou jumped onto the boarding plank. "Come on, Gregory!" he shouted at me, then he ran along it, just as Drake had.

I ran after him, telling myself it was just like the top of the Orchard wall at Whitehall—which is easy to walk along. The next thing I knew, we were crossing the Spanish deck and then climbing onto the Spaniard's boarding plank, to cross over to the *Arrow*.

And then, at last, we were scrambling onto the *Arrow*'s aft-deck. We pushed to the front of the crowd of sweaty sailors, and there was Captain Drake, pointing his pistol at Derby. There was blood on Drake's doublet, and his knuckles were grazed.

"All I want is a look in your Great Cabin, Derby," Drake was saying softly. "No more. We are old friends, and besides, you owe me that for taking the Spaniel for you."

Derby scowled. "What are you looking for?" he demanded. "There's no treasure in there. The booty's in the Spanish ship—bolts and bolts of silk that he must have had off a merchant."

"Ah, but I think there *is* a treasure in that cabin," said Drake. "Will I have to kill you to find it then, Derby? And you know I will, for all that we were friends once."

Derby scowled and then shrugged. "Good luck to you," he muttered. "She locked herself in last night, while we were busy trying to outsail the Spaniard, and she won't open up."

I nearly cheered.

"*She,* eh?" said Drake quietly.

"And her bloody tiring woman, too. I have had enough of the pair of them," Derby declared. He stepped up to the door of his cabin and banged on it. "Open up, you foolish woman, it's over!"

"No!" shrieked Lady Sarah's voice. "Take me back to the Queen—at once!" Only she said a lot more about Derby and his parents, which I am leaving out to save her reputation.

Drake smiled coldly. "So it's true, then. I counted you a friend, Hugh, for all we're so different. And you betrayed me! You stole a woman from the Queen's Court and had not the stomach to admit it, so you tried to lay the blame on me. I could have gone to the Tower and not even known why, thanks to you, *friend.*"

Derby stared at the deck.

Drake moved close to the cabin door, keeping Derby covered with his pistol. "Lady Sarah," he called, "it is Captain Francis Drake here, ma'am. Will you open to me? I've come for to take you back to Court."

There was silence. Then the door was unlatched and unbolted, and Lady Sarah peered out, with

Olwen beside her. They both looked very tired and dishevelled, and Lady Sarah's bright hair was tumbling down her back.

"I'll never marry you!" she screamed at Captain Derby. "How dare you abduct me and disparage me like this? I hope the Queen puts you in the Tower and hangs and draws and quarters you, you—"

Captain Drake stopped her furious tirade by raising his free hand. "My lady . . . ma'am," he said, "have you taken any hurt or . . . injury?"

"That man would have made me marry him last night," shouted Lady Sarah, "if Olwen and I had not knocked out his guard and barred the door when he went out on deck! And who knows what would have happened, if you had not come to rescue me, Captain Drake!"

Drake bowed, then looked around for me and Masou. "Indeed, you owe your thanks to your faithful friends, my lady: your page, Gregory, and his friend, Masou."

The Captain gestured for us to step forward.

I scowled at Lady Sarah, hoping and praying she wouldn't be too bone-headed and give away my true identity. "But that's not a pageboy!" she gasped. "That's—"

There was a sudden flurry. Captain Derby had

thrown himself at Sarah. Drake's gun fired, but Derby had moved too fast. Everyone froze again. Derby was backing away from Drake towards the rail. He had his fist tangled in Sarah's hair and his knife at her throat. She sobbed in fear.

"You'll lay down that pistol and get your men off my ship," he said to Drake, breathing fast. "And I'll be on my way with my Sarah, or no one shall marry her, ever."

Drake dropped his pistol to the deck, lifted his hands away from his sword belt, and stood quietly watching, his face focused and intent.

I could not bear the silence—I had to say something. "If you truly loved her, Captain Derby, you would let her go!" I burst out.

Derby blinked, and then stared at me. "What?"

"That is what true love is," I told him, and I knew it was true for my mother had taught me. "Not capturing her and threatening her and trying to marry her against her will. Let her go."

Derby looked confused for a second. Then he took his knife from Sarah's throat to point it at me. "One more word from you—"

There was a smooth movement from Drake—a bright flash through the air—and a horrible gristly thud! A knife was pinning Derby's right hand to the block next to his head. His own blade clattered to the floor. He stared disbelievingly at his wounded hand, then cried out with pain and shock.

Moments later, Sarah had stamped on his foot, wrenched his hand out of her hair, and taken refuge behind Drake.

Masou whistled and applauded.

"Now," said Drake, scooping his pistol off the deck again, "where's the First Mate of this ship?"

A stout man, who had been watching all the drama with interest, stepped forward. "Mr. Ketcham, sir," he said.

"Well, Mr. Ketcham, see the *Arrow* back to Tilbury—I'll not take her as a prize—we can talk about salvage later. I'll have your Captain and the Lady Sarah to my ship."

"Aye, sir."

There were wounded men to look after, and Derby's hand was freed from the block and roughly bandaged. He seemed to have lost all his energy and just stared at the deck listlessly. The Spaniards had already been rounded up and locked in their own hold by Mr. Newman and the boarding party, who were putting out the fires and setting the sails.

At last we all went back across the boarding

planks, with Lady Sarah holding onto Drake's arm and trembling. I ran across—because it is really much less frightening that way—and waited at the other end to help her down. As I did so, I whispered at her fiercely, "I'm Gregory, your pageboy! Until I say."

Sarah blinked at me, catching on slowly; at last she nodded. "Thank you, Gregory," she said, and smiled.

⌒

It was afternoon before everything was organized and the *Judith* was sailing back to the Thames mouth. At least a strong easterly wind had sprung up, which filled all the sails and made the ship lean over and plough through the water very fast. Lady Sarah and Olwen were nicely ensconced in Drake's Great Cabin, while Derby was in the brig.

At supper time Drake sent for me to attend on my lady, which I did, just as if I were serving the Queen. Lady Sarah sat at table with Drake, her hair still tumbling extravagantly down her back, and he blinked at her as if he found her too bright to look at.

"Will you tell me what happened to you, Lady

Sarah?" he asked at last, as I brought some boxes of sweetmeats for them to finish the meal.

"Oh, it was terrible!" Sarah began. "I knew Captain Derby was mooning after me a bit, but a lot of men do, you know. I didn't think anything much about it. And he never sent me a bracelet as you did, or wrote me a poem or anything. He just stood and stared. And then he sent me a message saying Olwen had met with an accident—"

"I hadn't, look you," interrupted Olwen. "And I got a message, supposedly from Lady Sarah, which asked me to collect a bag of pearls from a sea captain who had got some—"

"Which I never sent," put in Sarah. "Captain Derby forged my handwriting—"

"Well, I didn't think anything of it, and why would I?" continued Olwen's singsong voice. "So I went down to the watersteps, and the next thing I knew, two sailors had put a bag over my head, and no matter what I did, they trussed me up like a pig going to market. Well, I was in a terrible state, all the way down the river, and lying in the bottom of the boat, getting wet and—"

"They did it to use her as a hostage against me—" said Lady Sarah, drinking some more wine.

"And then they carried me onto a ship—and when

they took the bag off, there I was, trussed up in Captain Derby's Great Cabin, with an evil-looking ruffian holding a knife to my neck. I was terrified." Olwen ate two more marmelada sweetmeats and shook her head. "Quite terrified."

"I was already looking for Olwen to help me with my bodice when I got the message that she had had an accident," Lady Sarah continued. "I hurried to the stables, and when I arrived"—she popped a marmelada square in her mouth, too, and I sighed, because I love them and it looked as if she and Olwen between them were going to finish them all up—"there was Captain Derby, with some of his sailors. He told me he had Olwen on his ship and would do . . . awful things to her if I didn't come quietly with him. And his sailors would knife me if I screamed. So obviously, I fainted."

Obviously, I thought.

"When I came to again, Captain Derby was very impatient and not at all nice to me. He said I must come with him to the watersteps, or Olwen would die. But first I had to write a note to the Queen and another one to Captain Drake. I said I could not for I had sprained my right wrist when I fainted, and I cried about it (though it was not true)—so he had one of his men bandage my wrist, and hastily wrote the letters himself. Then he made me walk arm in arm with him down to the watersteps—and nobody noticed my plight at all—not young Robin, nor any of the tumblers." She pouted accusingly at Masou. "And I was in a terrible state, because he told me he was going to marry me, and I wouldn't dream of marrying a sea captain—even if my parents gave their consent, which they certainly would not. So all I could think of to do was give Robin a message that would not alert my captor, but which would alert those who know me. Everyone at Court knows that Lady Jane is no friend of mine!" Lady Sarah paused to draw breath, then she carried on. "We were rowed down the river to Captain Derby's ship. Once we were aboard, his crew made ready to weigh anchor, and Captain Derby sent a boy to take the other letter to Captain Drake, together with my pearl bracelet—which really seemed a most unnecessary gesture. And about an hour later we sailed from Tilbury."

"Aye," said Drake, "I was wondering why he was in such a hurry to leave—I thought he had heard word of a fine fat prize to take in the Narrow Seas, though I wasn't ready for sea myself."

"Masou and I saw the boy deliver the package to Captain Drake's ship, my lady," I put in. "If we had but known what was inside, we would have guessed your whereabouts all the sooner."

Lady Sarah nodded. "Captain Derby kept me and Olwen locked in the Great Cabin—which was very bad for Olwen, who got seasick. And that really was not too pleasant for me, either! He said his chaplain would marry us as soon as it was evening, and if I didn't say 'I do' he'd have me gagged, and the chaplain would hear whatever Derby told him to hear and then he'd cut off . . . he'd cut off Olwen's hands. . . ." Lady Sarah's voice trembled and two big glistening tears trickled down her face.

What a terrible thing to do to anybody, I thought. I tried to imagine what I'd do if somebody threatened to cut Ellie's hands off if I didn't marry him, and I thought I'd probably marry him, no matter how horrible he was. So all the nasty food, and fighting Tom—and even the sea battle—had really been in a good cause: to stop Derby's greedy selfish plans. I felt quite proud of Masou and myself.

Olwen put her arm around Lady Sarah and clucked over her. "Ah, now then, my lady, he didn't do it, so now."

Lady Sarah took a deep breath and shook her head. "And then there was a shout that they'd seen the Spanish ship sent out by the Duke of Alva—who is apparently a terrible pirate, and attacks any English and Dutch ships he can find. And then the Spanish ship started chasing us, which was even more frightening, so Captain Derby went out on deck. And while he was gone, I noticed that our guard had had quite a lot to drink, so I played cards with him and got him more drunk, and then Olwen crept up behind him and hit him on the head with a tray. Then we locked the door and barred the windows, so when Captain Derby came back with his chaplain, ready to marry me, he couldn't get in." Lady Sarah shook her head. "He was furious—and he called me so many evil names, I was quite sure I didn't want to marry such a raving bully.

"Olwen and I stayed up all night, to make sure he didn't break in—when he wasn't busy trying to sail away from the Spaniard, that is. And in the morning, there was cannon fire—which was terribly frightening—so we hid under the table. There was such a creaking and banging, and then a big roaring, clattering fight that went on and on! And finally, I heard *your* voice, Captain Drake!" she finished, fluttering her eyelashes at him. "I am *so* grateful to you!"

I had to choke back a laugh at that—typical Lady Sarah, I thought. There she was, just rescued from a fate worse than death—and still, she couldn't help flirting!

"I'll not take all the credit, my lady," said Drake with a tilt of his head. "Hugh Derby was one of my best friends. I would have trusted him with my life—my ship, even. The first I knew of what had happened to you was when your pageboy showed me the letter that was supposed to have come from you to the Queen, saying you were eloping with me. He's a good lad, my lady—I'd keep him by you if I was you. He slipped away from Court and crept onto the *Judith* because he thought I had you locked up here somewhere. And then, when he found out the truth, he came to me with the letter and told all he knew."

"But *you* did all the fighting to save me, didn't you, Captain?" Sarah gave Drake a dazzling smile. She didn't look grateful for all *my* hard work at all. And there was only one more marmelada sweetmeat left in the box, which I just knew she was going to take. And there it went. Typical!

"I'm always happy to fight—me and my crew with me." Drake grinned that ferocious piratical grin of his, and laughed. "It's a good Sunday's sport for us. And your young Gregory, and Masou, they fought from the top, shooting arrows and throwing fire

155

pots. They'll be fine men one day. If you have thanks to give for your rescue, you should reward them, too."

I felt myself blushing because I was so pleased to have Drake's respect. He is one of those people who makes you feel like a king—or a queen—if he praises you. I would far rather have his respect than any amount of cooing from Lady Sarah.

Sarah nodded to Masou and me—but then she looked down and sighed. "Though all is lost, anyway—for my reputation is now ruined," she said quietly. "I will have to marry a merchant—or even a lawyer."

I had to say something, so I bent on one knee, as a pageboy should, and said, "No, you won't, my lady. For nobody knows you've been gone."

Sarah blinked at me dimly. "Why not?" she asked.

"Because I've had Mary Shelton give out that you and—you have a quinsy and have been in bed," I explained.

"You have? Really?" Sarah said incredulously, her face brightening.

"Yes, my lady. All we have to do is smuggle you back into the palace without anyone noticing, and then to our—your chamber, and nobody will ever know what happened."

Lady Sarah clapped her hands and laughed in delight. "Are you sure?"

"So long as you and Olwen don't tell anybody," I added, knowing Lady Sarah.

"Why, that's a wonderful idea." Then her face fell. "Except it means that Derby won't go to the Tower for abducting me."

Drake poured Lady Sarah some more wine. "I'll free him when we get to Tilbury," he told her. "It's not justice, right enough, but I doubt he'll set sail in his own ship again, for he was in debt to fit out the *Arrow,* and she'll need a new mast and yards as well. He'll have to sell her, and then the only way he can set to sea is sailing as someone else's mate or purser."

"You sound sorry for him, Captain Drake," said Lady Sarah, a little petulantly.

"I *am* sorry for him, even though he betrayed our friendship and tried to have me blamed for his crime," Drake replied. "By his own fault and sinfulness he has lost the finest thing a man can have."

"A wife," said Olwen knowingly to Lady Sarah.

Drake looked puzzled. "No, a ship," he corrected.

Lady Sarah and Olwen both looked a little put out at that. They were used to courtly gentlemen, after all.

Drake waved a hand, completely unaware of this. "When you're master of your own ship, you're as free as the wind. You can set sail upon a day, and go all round the world, visiting strange and wonderful lands—and all the time you are in your own house, with your household around you."

"Will you ever marry, Captain Drake?" Lady Sarah asked, a little flirtatiously.

"Aye." He smiled at her. "I'm minded to ask Mr. Newman for his daughter's hand, for she's a pretty little thing, and used to sailors—and I've the money to keep a wife like her, now."

Sarah now looked *very* put out. "Oh," she said pointedly. "You are not ambitious in your choice of wife, then?"

I saw Drake's blue eyes turn sharp, and thought, You have lost him now, Lady Sarah—if ever you truly had him.

Drake laughed. "Ambitious? Not for a wife wealthier and of higher blood than me, no. But ambitious to sail about the world and take satisfaction in blood from the treacherous Spaniards? Yes. That I am." He put his silver goblet down with a sharp tap and stood up. "Now, ladies, I know you must be weary from watching all night, and in need of rest. I'll bunk down in the Mate's cabin, and I desire you to make yourself free with anything you need in here."

Sarah nodded her thanks. "Oh, and Captain," she trilled, "may we have Masou and Gr—egory, to guard us in the night?"

Drake frowned. "You are in no danger on this ship, my lady," he said.

Sarah's eyes opened wide. "From the mice, Captain. There were dreadfully big ones on Derby's ship, you know."

Drake shook his head and chuckled. "Of course," he said. "Gregory and Masou, you stay here—and behave yourselves, or I'll give you what for in the morning."

"Aye, Captain," said Masou and I together, nearly dying of trying not to laugh.

"Goodnight, ladies," said Drake as he went to the door. "By the early hours of the morning, with this wind and God willing, we'll be in Tilbury." And he bowed courteously.

Lady Sarah and Olwen curtsied back. I caught myself just in time, and bowed like Masou.

As soon as the Captain had shut the door behind

him, Masou and I fell on the remains of the dinner. I don't think I'd like to be a pageboy. It's agony watching people gobble up all the sweetmeats when you're really hungry for one.

"Grace?" asked Lady Sarah, not sounding quite sure. "Is it really Grace?"

"Mmph," I said, nodding. My mouth was full of game pie.

Olwen stared at me, gave a little shriek, and sat down suddenly. "What . . . ?" she gasped. "What have you done with your hair?"

Honestly! What a daft question. "I cut it off, of course," I said impatiently.

"Is it true, what Captain Drake said you did, Grace?" Lady Sarah asked incredulously. "You came to find me, and you were in the battle?"

I nodded. "Well, high up above it," I dismissed, not wanting Lady Sarah to make her usual fuss. "And Masou was there, too, of course."

"Oh," said Lady Sarah, shaking her head. "How extraordinary. . . . Was it very hard work?"

I thought about this. "Yes," I said, "it was. So— are there any more marmelada sweetmeats?"

As we were arranging the little cabin for the night, there came a knock on the door. The Boatswain entered, carrying a basket. He was smiling fondly.

160

"Now then, m'dears, these here ladies'll take care of you . . . ," he said—which puzzled me until I realized he was talking to something in the basket.

He put it on the table and Sarah and Olwen peered in, then started to coo and exclaim. I peeked, too, and saw the mother cat and her kittens, now looking much happier. The kittens were asleep, with their paws curled on their fat little tummies, and the mother cat was purring.

"She'm the maddest cat I ever saw! Fancy her taking her kittens all the way up the mast! Tom fetched her down," said the Boatswain, who now didn't seem nearly so fierce. "Can you take care of her, ladies?" he asked. "She's a fine ratter, and her kittens are shaping well, what's more."

It was a silly question, really. Nobody could resist them, and soon they were in the warmest, safest corner, with Olwen feeding the mother scraps of meat-pie filling and Sarah dangling a bit of thread to see if the kittens would play.

We did sleep a little, me and Sarah sharing the little cot, and Olwen on a pallet, with poor Masou by the door. But we had to wake up again at about two in the morning because we were nearly there.

As we sailed back into Tilbury, Drake had his gig ready to go up the Thames, and we came to

Greenwich watersteps before it was light. Obviously, the great watergate was closed and locked, but there was a boat unloading loaves of bread by the kitchen steps already.

Lady Sarah and Olwen were muffled up in cloaks, and I led them in—still disguised as a page—telling the Yeoman that they were friends visiting Lady Sarah. I could tell he didn't believe me, though. He probably thought there was something scandalous going on with the courtiers.

We went through some of the rarely used back passages that Masou knew of, and slipped into our own bedchamber, while Masou kept watch. Then he went off to his own sleeping place to rest.

"I am utterly exhausted," Sarah said loudly, as Olwen helped her off with her stays. "I am sure it will take me several days to recover from such a terrible ordeal."

Mary Shelton woke up, and sighed in relief when she saw that we had all returned safely. She was looking quite ill herself, with red eyes and bags under them as well.

Ellie awoke, too, and sat up looking ever so much better—no fever, rosy cheeks. I'd say she was even a little less thin.

Mary climbed out of bed. "What happened to you, Grace?" she demanded, clasping her hands. "Where have you been? I was so desperately *worried*! I've been praying and praying for your safe return. I nearly went and told the Queen when you weren't back by last night!"

"Good thing I had the sense to stop you, eh?" said Ellie. "I know Grace." She gave me a big hug, and squawked with laughter at how I looked with my hair short, and in boys' clothes. I took them off and bundled them up for her to take back to the tumblers' tiring room. Then I changed my shift and got into bed, with every bone in my body aching with relief and tiredness.

Mary Shelton was so kind, she even said she'd wait to hear the whole story until I had slept. And then my eyes closed by themselves, as Lady Sarah got on with telling of her adventures.

⸺

Before I knew it, it was midday and Mary Shelton was shaking me awake for dinner. She had brought a tray of food, which we demolished. I was absolutely starving, and even Ellie was impressed at how much I ate.

I have spent the afternoon writing everything I

could remember of my adventures in my daybooke. After all, I was ill with a quinsy, wasn't I? And so was Lady Sarah. It was essential that nobody find out where Sarah had really been, for even though she was kidnapped and taken against her will, her reputation would still be ruined if the truth came out. So we stayed in our chamber and let it be known that we couldn't possibly attend the Queen when we were both still so ill.

When I'd written down my adventures (thank goodness I'd been able to make some notes or I'd never have remembered everything), I read selected bits out to Mary and Ellie, and Sarah and Olwen, and they laughed and gasped and oohed, just as if I were a proper storyteller.

By then, Ellie was so much better that, when the coast was clear, she crept out of the bedchamber and went back to the laundry.

Mary Shelton went to fetch my Uncle Cavendish this evening, so that he could examine Sarah and me, and pronounce us recovered from the quinsy. He came and looked at our throats, felt our pulses and foreheads—then solemnly pronounced our quinsies quite abated, thanks to his care.

Masou came creeping in to see us, too, and I had to read my account to them all again, with Masou adding comments when he thought I had forgotten something important. Mary, Sarah, and Olwen all listened and gasped in disbelief and clapped. I've even started to wonder myself if I really did all that— did I really climb a mast, fight in a battle?

I think Her Majesty is wonderful, the way she understands.

This morning Mrs. Champernowne came bustling in: Sarah and I were to attend the Queen in the Presence Chamber, now we had been pronounced well again.

Lady Sarah helped me to pin up my short hair with a hairpiece, to make it look as if I still had it long, and then, damasked and pearled, off we all went to the Presence.

Lady Jane gasped when she saw Lady Sarah, who ignored her with great aplomb as she sailed past. "Are you recovered of your illness now, dear Lady Sarah?" she asked.

"Yes, thank you," said Sarah. "My quinsy is quite gone."

"It has been very quiet without you." Lady Jane's arched eyebrows went up a bit when she said this.

"How kind of you to say so . . ." Sarah was positively simpering.

The trumpets blared and we all rose to curtsy and dispose ourselves neatly. Her Majesty was staring hard at me—which worried me a little—but then she smiled, and I thought she probably wasn't angry.

And then in came Captain Drake himself, followed by Mr. Newman, who was carrying a bolt of beautiful samite silk, which he placed in front of the Queen on the dais.

"Your Majesty," said the Captain with a bow. "With your permission, I would like to present this bolt of silk to my Lady Sarah Bartelmy, as a compensation for the gown that was ruined when she fell—" He'd turned to smile at Lady Sarah, and seen me sitting demurely with my needlework. "That was . . . er . . . ruined by sea water . . ." He trailed off, still staring at me.

"Ah yes, Captain," the Queen replied smoothly, "perhaps you remember my Lady Grace Cavendish, our youngest Maid of Honour. She turned the winch for the most notable contest between the Spanish galleon and the purposed English race-built ship." And she gestured for me to come forward.

I stood up and went to Her Majesty.

Drake looked from me to the Queen and his

mouth was opening and shutting like a codfish. "She . . . ah . . . Do you have a brother, my lady?" he asked.

I curtsied to him and looked demurely at the floor. "No, sir, I am an only child."

"Perhaps a cousin named Gregory?" he pressed.

"No, sir." I stared straight up at those vivid blue eyes and I couldn't resist it. I winked. Then I looked at the Queen, who had a very peculiar expression on her face—half disapproval, half amusement. She knows! I thought at once.

I'd wager all London to a turnip that, last eventide, Captain Drake had told Her Majesty the tale of what happened, as a wild romantical sea captain's tall tale. The Queen will have formed her own conclusions about that enterprising pageboy, Gregory. And she dearly loves to tease a handsome man.

"Ah . . . And what have you been doing these last few days, my lady?" Captain Drake asked me, recovering swiftly.

"Oh, sir, I have been in bed with a terrible quinsy," I replied, and then felt reckless: "Why, I had such a fever I dreamed I was in a sea battle and that a cat brought her kittens up to the fighting top while the cannons were firing!" Just for a second I caught the Queen's eye and nearly ruined all by laughing—for I could see that she was near to bursting, too.

The Queen can be most subtle and tactful when she wants. She would have stopped me going if she had known in advance, just as Ellie said, and I would have been in terrible trouble if I had been caught. But to bring off such a venture with no mishap, and save Lady Sarah from disgrace as well—that pleased her. If ever she should ask me whether I was Gregory, I will tell her the truth, of course. But I'll wager she never will—and will be most careful not to find out about it, either . . . *officially*.

Drake was staring at me, blue eyes boring into mine—but I didn't mind a bit, and just stared him right back. I'm a Maid of Honour. Only a madman would accuse a Maid of Honour of being in a sea battle.

Suddenly Drake shouted with laughter and bowed to me and the Queen together. "By God, Your Majesty," he said. "By God, when we have Maids of Honour such as these in England, no wonder all the world is in awe of us!"

And for the rest of the audience, while the Queen thanked him for his gift of treasure and a prize ship for the rebuilding of the Navy, he would look at me every so often, and grin suddenly, like a boy.

Meanwhile, Lady Sarah sat with a satisfied little smile on her face like a cat at a cream bowl, while Lady Jane scowled down at her blackwork with a face of thunder.

And I smiled secretly to myself, for here was another mystery successfully unravelled by Her Majesty's own Lady Pursuivant—with not a little help from Masou—and Gregory the page, of course. . . .

alchemist—a name given to a kind of chemist who sought to turn ordinary metals into gold. Some alchemists also sought the key to eternal life and a universal cure for disease.

Allah akhbar—an Islamic war cry. It means "God is great."

Allemayne—Germany

aqua vitae—brandy

banshee—a spirit in Irish folklore well known for wailing loudly

Bedlam—the major asylum for the insane in London during Elizabethan times—the name came from the Hospital of St. Mary of Bethlehem

biggin cap—a child's hat

blackwork—black embroidery on white linen

bracer—an arm or wrist protector used by an archer

brig—a small ship with two square-rigged sails, often used for piracy *brocade*—a rich, gold-embroidered fabric

bumroll—a sausage-shaped piece of padding worn round the hips to make them look bigger

buttery—confusingly, this was where barrels of beer, wine, and brandy were kept for people to fetch drinks from

cable tiers—the area on a ship where the anchor chain (or cable) was stored

capstan—a large winch, often used for hauling up the anchor or anything else that was particularly heavy

Chamberer—a servant of the Queen who cleaned her chamber for her, which the Maids of Honour and Ladies-in-Waiting, of course, could not be expected to do

citron—a citrus fruit similar to a lemon but with a very thick rind

close-stool—a portable toilet comprising a seat with a hole in it on top of a box with a chamber pot inside

Cloth of Estate—a kind of awning that went over the Queen's chair to indicate that she was the Queen

Clown's All-Heal—a plant, also known as St. John's wort

codpiece—a flap or bag that concealed the opening in the front of a man's breeches *copper*—usually a copper saucepan or cauldron used for cooking

damask—a beautiful, self-patterned silk cloth woven in Flanders. It originally came from Damascus—hence the name.

daybooke—a book in which you would record your sins each day so that you could pray about them. The idea of keeping a diary or journal grew out of this. Grace uses her daybooke as a journal.

dottle—partly burned tobacco in the bowl of a pipe

doublet—a close-fitting padded jacket worn by men

Duke of Alva—the Spanish ruler in the Netherlands during Elizabethan times

false front—a pretty piece of material sewn to the front of a plain petticoat so that it would show under the kirtle

farthingale—a bell- or barrel-shaped petticoat held out with hoops of whalebone

fighting top—a platform halfway up a ship's mast where a Navy man could stand and shoot

fire pot—a clay pot, filled with material that would easily catch fire, used as a missile in battle and to carry hot coals

fletching—the feathers on an arrow

forecastle—the foremost part of the upper deck of a ship

French cut—fashionably tight and curvy

galleon—a heavy square-rigged sailing ship used for war or trade, especially by the Spanish

galley—the area of a ship where the crew's meals were cooked. In Elizabethan times the galley was deep down in the ship's bilges, where there was maximum stability and where the cooking fire could be put out easily if necessary.

gig—a long, narrow rowing boat

grappling irons—large hooks on ropes. These were thrown from one ship onto another to pull it closer so that it could be boarded and captured.

Habsburg—the family name of Philip II and one of the great ruling dynasties of Europe

halberd—a weapon consisting of a battle-axe and pike mounted on a long handle

harbinger—a courtier who went ahead to announce the monarch

henbane of Peru—also known as tobacco. In Elizabethan times it was regarded as a great cure for phlegm.

Henchman—a young serving man, often related to the person he was serving. His work might well involve acting as a bodyguard.

hose—tight-fitting cloth trousers worn by men

jakes—an Elizabethan term for an outside toilet

jerkin—a close-fitting, hip-length, usually sleeveless jacket

kirtle—the skirt section of an Elizabethan dress

Lady-in-Waiting—one of the ladies who helped look after the Queen and who kept her company

lateen—a narrow, triangular sail on a very long yard set at an angle to the mast

lye—a strongly alkaline ingredient in soap

Maid of Honour—a younger girl who helped to look after the Queen like a Lady-in-Waiting

man-of-war—a warship

marmelada—a very thick jammy sweet often made from quinces

Mary Shelton—one of Queen Elizabeth's Maids of Honor (a Maid of Honor of this name really did exist; see below). Most Maids of Honor were not officially "Ladies" (like Lady Grace), but they had to be born of gentry.

merchant venturer—a person who invested in overseas trade

merchanter or *merchantman*—a trading ship

Muscovy—the kingdom of Moscow; Old Russia

Mussulman—an old name for a Muslim

Narrow Seas—the English Channel

New Spain—South America

New World—South and North America together

on progress—a term used when the Queen was touring parts of her realm. Such travel was a kind of summer holiday for her.

Parlour—a room off the Hall that was just beginning to be used for eating, among other things

penner—a small leather case that would attach to a belt. It was used for holding quills, ink, knife, and any other equipment needed for writing.

pitch—a black substance similar to tar

poop deck—a deck right at the stern of a ship

popinjay—a parrot

posset—a hot drink made from sweetened and spiced milk curdled with ale or wine

potherbs—vegetables

pottage—a thick soup

Presence Chamber—the room where Queen Elizabeth would receive people

Privy Garden—Queen Elizabeth's private garden

pursuivant—one who pursues someone else

Queen's Guard—these were more commonly known as the Gentlemen Pensioners, young noblemen who guarded the Queen from physical attacks

quinsy—very bad tonsillitis

raiment—clothing

Royal Standard—Queen Elizabeth's flag (*not* the Union Jack) *samite*—a heavy satin fabric

sea beggars—a derogatory term for the Dutch rebels who fought the Spanish at sea

Secretary to the Admiralty—the man in charge of the Navy (as it existed then)

shipworm—teredo worm; a wood-boring beetle that rendered most ships unusable after twenty years, until copper-bottoming came in during the eighteenth century

shipwright—a carpenter expert in shipbuilding and repair

slow match—rope soaked in saltpeter to make it burn slowly and steadily

snips—an early form of scissors without the pivot—a little like small sheep shears

Spaniels—a mispronunciation of *Espagnols* (*Spanish*) by the English

statute cap—a blue woollen cap worn by all apprentices to support the woollen industry

stays—the boned, laced bodice worn around the body under the clothes. Victorians called the stays a corset.

sterncastle—the back of a warship, built up to allow the crew to board other ships

stomacher—a heavily embroidered or jeweled piece for the center front of a bodice *tinder box*—small box containing some quick-burning tinder, a piece of flint, a piece of steel, and a candle for making fire and thus light

tiring room—a room for dressing or changing clothes in

tiring woman—a woman who helped a lady to dress

topman—the aristocrats of the lower deck, these were the sailors who worked high up on the mast and in the yards

tumbler—an acrobat

vein or *open a vein*—a cut made in a vein to let out "bad" blood. This was used as a cure for almost anything!

Verge of the Court—anywhere within a mile of the Queen's person

vittles—food

waterman—a man who rowed a ferry boat on the Thames; he was a kind of Elizabethan cabdriver

watersteps—steps leading down to the river

wherry—a Thames boat

willow-bark tincture—a solution made from willow bark, which was good for pain relief but very bad for the stomach. It was later developed into aspirin.

Withdrawing Chamber—the Queen's private rooms

yard—a long pole on which a sail hangs

Forget everything you thought you knew about sea battles and pirates, because in Elizabethan times, war at sea wasn't as clear-cut as you might imagine!

In the sixteenth century there were no naval uniforms, no press gangs (men who later forced civilians into joining the army and navy), and only a few purpose-built warships, which often doubled as privateer vessels. A privateer was a pirate who preyed upon the ships of one or two countries, as allowed by his sovereign in a letter of marque.

At this time, the Royal Navy was basically a random collection of privateers and armed merchants who volunteered to serve the Queen whenever it was necessary. Very often they weren't paid unless they captured another ship, and then they received prize money for it.

Later in Elizabeth's reign, Sir Francis Drake was one of the most successful of these pirates—with investments from the Queen as well as many of her courtiers. The early Elizabethan ships were quite primitive, but the technology was evolving at a tremendous rate. And when the Armada came in 1588, it was thanks to the race-built galleons—designed by John Hawkins—that the English ships were able to outsail and outgun the Spanish.

In 1485, Queen Elizabeth I's grandfather, Henry Tudor, won the battle of Bosworth Field against Richard III and took the throne of England. He was known as Henry VII. He had two sons, Arthur and Henry. Arthur died while still a boy, so when Henry VII died in 1509, Elizabeth's father came to the throne and England got an eighth king called Henry—the notorious one who had six wives.

Wife number one—Catherine of Aragon—gave Henry one daughter called Mary (who was brought up as a Catholic) but no living sons. To Henry VIII this was a disaster, because nobody believed a queen could ever govern England. He needed a male heir.

Henry wanted to divorce Catherine so he could marry his pregnant mistress, Anne Boleyn. The Pope, the head of the Catholic Church, wouldn't allow him to annul his marriage, so Henry broke with the Catholic Church and set up the Protestant

Church of England—or the Episcopal Church, as it's known in the United States.

Wife number two—Anne Boleyn—gave Henry another daughter, Elizabeth (who was brought up as a Protestant). When Anne then miscarried a baby boy, Henry decided he'd better get somebody new, so he accused Anne of infidelity and had her executed.

Wife number three—Jane Seymour—gave Henry a son called Edward and died of childbed fever a couple of weeks later.

Wife number four—Anne of Cleves—had no children. It was a diplomatic marriage and Henry didn't fancy her, so she agreed to a divorce (wouldn't you?).

Wife number five—Catherine Howard—had no children, either. Like Anne Boleyn, she was accused of infidelity and executed.

Wife number six—Catherine Parr—also had no children. She did manage to outlive Henry, though, but only by the skin of her teeth. Nice guy, eh?

Henry VIII died in 1547, and in accordance with the rules of primogeniture (whereby the firstborn son inherits from his father), the person who succeeded him was the boy Edward. He became Edward VI. He was strongly Protestant but died young, in 1553.

Next came Catherine of Aragon's daughter, Mary, who became Mary I, known as Bloody Mary. She was strongly Catholic, married Philip II of Spain in a diplomatic match, but died childless five years later. She also burned a lot of Protestants for the good of their souls.

Finally, in 1558, Elizabeth came to the throne. She reigned until her death in 1603. She played the marriage game—that is, she kept a lot of important and influential men hanging on in hopes of marrying her—for a long time. At one time it looked as if she would marry her favorite, Robert Dudley, Earl of Leicester. She didn't, though, and I think she probably never intended to get married—would you, if you'd had a dad like hers? So she never had any children.

She was an extraordinary and brilliant woman, and during her reign, England first started to become important as a world power. Sir Francis Drake sailed round the world—raiding the Spanish colonies of South America for loot as he went. And one of Elizabeth's favorite courtiers, Sir Walter Raleigh, tried to plant the first English colony in North America—at the site of Roanoke in 1585. It failed, but the idea stuck.

The Spanish King Philip II tried to conquer

England in 1588. He sent a huge fleet of 150 ships, known as the Invincible Armada, to do it. It failed miserably—defeated by Drake at the head of the English fleet—and most of the ships were wrecked trying to sail home. There were many other great Elizabethans, too—including William Shakespeare and Christopher Marlowe.

After her death, Elizabeth was succeeded by James VI of Scotland, who became James I of England and Scotland. He was almost the last eligible person available! He was the son of Mary, Queen of Scots, who was Elizabeth's cousin, via Henry VIII's sister.

James's son was Charles I—the king who was beheaded after losing the English Civil War.

The stories about Lady Grace Cavendish are set in the year 1569, when Elizabeth was thirty-six and still playing the marriage game for all she was worth. The Ladies-in-Waiting and Maids of Honor at her Court weren't servants—they were companions and friends, supplied from upper-class families. Not all of them were officially "Ladies"—only those with titled husbands or fathers; in fact, many of them were unmarried younger daughters sent to Court to find themselves a nice rich lord to marry.

All the Lady Grace Mysteries are invented, but some of the characters in the stories are real people—Queen Elizabeth herself, of course, and Mrs. Champernowne and Mary Shelton as well. There never was a Lady Grace Cavendish (as far as we know!)—but there were plenty of girls like her at Elizabeth's Court. The real Mary Shelton foolishly made fun of the Queen herself on one occasion—and got slapped in the face by Elizabeth for her trouble! But most of the time, the Queen seems to have been protective of and kind to her Maids of Honor. She was very strict about boyfriends, though. There was one simple rule for boyfriends in those days: you couldn't have one. No boyfriends at all. You would get married to a person your parents chose for you and that was that. Of course, the girls often had other ideas!

Later on in her reign, the Queen had a full-scale secret service run by her great spymaster, Sir Francis Walsingham. His men, who hunted down priests and assassins, were called Pursuivants. There are also tantalizing hints that Elizabeth may have had her own personal sources of information—she certainly was very well informed, even when her counselors tried to keep her in the dark. And who knows whom she might have recruited to find things out for her? There may even have been a Lady Grace Cavendish, after all!

Be on the lookout

for the next

Lady Grace Mystery,

CONSPIRACY,

on sale

in February 2005.

Turn the page

for a special preview.

Conspiracy

*At Baron Oxey his house, in the County
of Oxfordshire—shortly before sunrise*

We are just making ready to leave Oxey Hall.
And here have I another daybooke and five fine new
quill pens from the feathers of one of the geese, and
the Queen has given me a new bottle full of ink,
made with crystal and chased with gold, and it has a
stopper that locks. She gave it me on condition I do
no more writing when wearing my white damask
gown. Not even if I am very careful. We have
unpicked the piece that somehow got ink upon it
and put a new piece of white damask in—I think it
looks very well, though Mrs. Champernowne grum-
bled that the colour was a little different.

I am writing this as I sit upon a big chest full of

clothes, wearing my black wool kirtle, which will take no harm from ink at all, so fie on you, Mrs. Champernowne.

Olwen, Lady Sarah's tiring woman, is trying to pack all Sarah's little pots of face paint and unguents, but Lady Sarah keeps unpacking them again. She has a new spot on her chin, and she is searching for an ointment her mother gave her yestereven—of goose fat with a burnt mouse's tail mixed in it—sovereign against all blemishes.

Mary Shelton is nibbling at some gingerbread and watching. "Did you never think that perhaps it is all the creams and elixirs you use that give you so many spots, Sarah?" she just asked.

Sarah only tossed her head and made a "*Ptah!*" noise, though I think Mary has a point.

When we leave the Oxeys' house, the Court will move to Kenilworth, which is my lord the Earl of Leicester's chief residence—the Queen gave it him five years ago. It is very exciting—my lord of Leicester is Master of the Queen's Horse and her best friend and he organizes all the revels and processions and ceremonies for the Court and so we are looking forward to wonderful entertainments at his own residence. My tumbler friend Masou will be performing. He has already gone ahead to make ready.

I love being on progress. Although it is tiresome to have to share a chamber with all five of the other Maids of Honour. Lady Sarah constantly fusses over her face paint—of course, I am used to that—and bickers with Lady Jane Coningsby. Carmina Willoughby and Penelope Knollys gossip incessantly like noisy geese. And Mary Shelton, with whom I share a bed, snores most horribly and keeps me awake half the night. Nevertheless, even if it were not a way for the Queen to see her people, feed the Court at the expense of her nobles, and allow the London palaces to be cleaned and whitewashed, going on progress would still be the finest way to spend the hot summer months when London is full of plague.

I don't even mind all the riding from one house to another with the rest of the Court cavalcade, because all of us Maids of Honour ride nice steady amblers and we each sit behind a groom on pillion seats. Lady Jane Coningsby, who is a good rider, complains that it is too tedious for words, but I feel much better with another controlling the horse. Somehow, whatever I ask a horse to do, I find it always does the opposite.

The Queen says I am too soft with my horse and do not make it obey me, and that is why my mounts always act so froward and unseat me—or run away with me!

Lady Sarah is now squinting to put on her spot cream by the light of one small candle. As her creams usually do, it smells very nasty despite having heal-all pounded into it as well as the mouse-tail ashes.

My dear friend Ellie, the laundrymaid, just went by with her arms full of sheets and rolled her eyes at me over Sarah. One of the best things about being on progress is that I can borrow Ellie from the laundry and have her with me as my unofficial tiring woman. She is currently making herself useful by helping Olwen pile the sheets into chests, while Olwen mutters to herself, "Wherefore six sheets and nine smocks and every one of them used? Ah, bless you, Ellie, they can all pack here, look you, and then we shall have space for the pillowcases. . . ."

One of the men from the Removing Wardrobe of Beds has begun to take down the bed curtains. Usually they wait until we are all gone but they want to be off soon. The Removing Wardrobe has two sets of everything, so while we are in Kenilworth they will be going to our next destination and setting everything up again ready for the Queen.

Now the other two men are on ladders, unpegging

the tester-frame and the posts, and carrying bed parts through the passageways and out into the courtyard. I can see the carts waiting by torchlight, with the horses still munching in their nosebags and stamping their huge hairy feet.

The Queen's Chambers are the last to go. The men always wait until she is gone before they start dismantling them and taking down the frames of brocade from the walls. When everything is ready we will go and attend upon her. Oh, no, not again! Sarah picked up another pot—with ground talcum in it this time—and a swansdown puff to carefully powder the end of her nose.

"Will you kindly be giving me that, my lady?" Olwen snapped, picking up the pot and holding her hand out for the puff. "You shall be late for attending upon Her Majesty, look you. . . ."

"But my nose is all shiny again," Sarah said with a pout. "I'll just—"

Olwen has just tutted and nipped the swansdown puff out of Sarah's fingers, because Mrs. Champernowne, Mistress of the Maids, has come bustling in.

"Where are the Maids of Honour?" she is saying. "Come along with you, now. You should have been ready to attend Her Majesty ten minutes ago!"

And so I must put my beautiful new daybooke and my penner away in my embroidery bag to attend the Queen—I wonder what she will be like today. She hates mornings but she loves progresses, so it is like tossing a coin.

—

Suspicion and Bloodshed!

The Royal Court is on its summer travels and Lady Grace is sure something strange is going on. As Queen Elizabeth narrowly escapes a series of mysterious accidents, Grace must investigate just who might be behind the conspiracy. Could it really be one of the Queen's faithful friends—or even her latest suitor?

Delve into the daybooke of Lady Grace, Queen Elizabeth's favorite Maid of Honor, to discover a deadly dangerous plot. . . .

Conspiracy

Available everywhere February 2005

Excerpt copyright © 2005 by Working Partners Ltd. Published by Delacorte Press, an imprint of Random House Children's Books, a division of Random House, Inc.